**His fingers closed around Ava's wrist and her pulse jumped and raced.**

"I don't know why we feel something and it comes out of the blue," he said.

"I've never had it happen with a complete stranger who doesn't even know his name," she whispered, and he flashed that smile that made her heart pound. Only inches were between them and his gaze held hers and she couldn't breathe.

"Damn, I can't resist when you get me wound up with a look. I know full well you don't even want to have that effect."

"No, I don't," she whispered. They stared at each other. She couldn't move or look away.

"You don't want to step away any more than I want to. Just say to hell with it," he whispered and closed the last tiny bit of distance between them.

Then he took her into his arms and kissed her.

\* \* \*

*In Bed with the Rancher* by Sara Orwig is part of the Return of the Texas Heirs series.

Dear Reader,

This story begins when Ava Carter, an occupational therapist who has her own Dallas company, is in the Texas Hill Country, where she has a cabin. After getting supplies in a small town, she is caught in torrential rain on her way to her cabin. Ahead, as a pickup spins off the road, a man jumps out. She stops and gets him into her car. When he jumped, the man hit his head and lost his memory. She has a neighbor who is a good friend, and he comes to meet the stranger.

Days later, through the neighbor friend's contacting the sheriff, they learn the stranger's identity is Wynn Sterling. From the first hour, Ava and Wynn fight an instant and intense attraction. He doesn't want to get involved with anyone when he can't remember who he is or anything about himself. And she doesn't want to fall in love with him for the same reasons, but the hot attraction is impossible to resist.

When the storm subsides and she can take him to his Dallas home, they both wonder what lies ahead. Shocks, a jealous twin and other upheavals are in their lives as love grows with their future, a rocky road of uncertainties.

Books have filled my life with hours of entertainment. I hope you enjoy reading this book.

Thank you,

*Sara Orwig*

# SARA ORWIG

—

# IN BED WITH THE RANCHER

HARLEQUIN
DESIRE

# HARLEQUIN®
## DESIRE™

ISBN-13: 978-1-335-20927-6

In Bed with the Rancher

Copyright © 2020 by Sara Orwig

This edition published by arrangement with Harlequin Books S.A.

For questions and comments about the quality of this book, please contact us at CustomerService@Harlequin.com.

Harlequin Enterprises ULC
22 Adelaide St. West, 40th Floor
Toronto, Ontario M5H 4E3, Canada
www.Harlequin.com

Married to the guy she met in college, *USA TODAY* bestselling author **Sara Orwig** has three children and six grandchildren. Sara has published 109 novels. One of the first six inductees into the Oklahoma Professional Writers Hall of Fame, Sara has twice won Oklahoma Novel of the Year. Sara loves family, friends, dogs, books, beaches and Dallas, Texas.

### Books by Sara Orwig

### Harlequin Desire

#### *Callahan's Clan*

*Expecting the Rancher's Child*
*The Rancher's Baby Bargain*
*The Rancher's Cinderella Bride*
*The Texan's Baby Proposal*

#### *Texas Promises*

*Expecting a Lone Star Heir*
*The Forbidden Texan*
*The Rancher's Heir*

#### *Return of the Texas Heirs*

*In Bed with the Rancher*

Visit her Author Profile page at Harlequin.com, or saraorwig.com, for more titles.

You can also find Sara Orwig on Facebook, along with other Harlequin Desire authors, at Facebook.com/harlequindesireauthors!

To Stacy Boyd with endless thanks for all you do.

# One

Driving north on the back roads of Texas, Wade Sterling was trying to get away from a storm.

He'd been on the Gulf, fishing, when the weather had cut his trip short. He'd received warnings of violent storms developing farther out in the Gulf and heading toward the coast. He had docked near Corpus Christi and was now driving north. When he had a little more distance between him and the coast, he would turn east to get onto Interstate 45 North into Dallas.

He had called home and told his mother he was safely back on land and he would be home in a few days, maybe even a week. He had learned long ago to overestimate how long he'd be gone or she'd get worried. He suspected he would be caught in rain driving home, so the trip might take longer than usual.

Now, however, the forecast called for possible flooding. To keep his mind off the weather, he thought about things he needed to do when he got home. Before he drove to Bar S Ranch, he wanted to stop at his condo in Dallas. He needed to go by his office because he had real estate holdings he should check on and other business matters to attend to.

He and his rancher cousins, Cal Brand, Jake Reed and Luke Grayson, had all contributed money to build a new arena in Fort Worth to replace a popular old arena that had burned down. The city wanted a grand opening and he and his cousins needed to agree on a date. He should get with his cousins and get that date settled.

Sadness gripped him when he thought about his cousin, Cal. Cal had been a rancher, as the rest of them were, but he wanted life on the wild side, too. He had done undercover work for the government. He'd said two more years and he would retire to his ranch. When Wade contacted Cal about donating to build the new arena, Cal was enthusiastic and sent more than they'd planned, saying he was sure the builders would find a use for the money. Two months later, his family received word that Cal had died in an accident on the Atlantic Ocean. The surviving cousins attended the memorial service held by Cal's family. Wade shook his head. He would miss Cal who was interesting, fun, and a good rancher.

Another of Wade's cousins had had a sad event. It

was two years ago when Luke's wife and baby boy were killed in a car wreck. Luke no longer was as light-hearted as he had been before losing his family and Wade could understand why. It made him sad and he wondered if Luke would ever be the happy person he once was.

A deep rumble of thunder warned Wade he wasn't going to beat the storm.

His thoughts shifted to getting home.

Which led to thoughts of Olivia, and his need to break things off with her.

Though she was beautiful and exciting to be with, she was getting too serious. He didn't want to marry—not ever. Problem was, she did, and she made it obvious. Just the thought of marriage sent a chill down his spine. He never wanted to marry and risk having a kid like his twin. His identical twin. Identical in looks but not in temperament and personality. Not at all. Wynn had caused trouble as far back as Wade could remember.

Wade thought about the latest example. Last month, when he had stopped by his parents' home and waited for their return from the grocer's, their landline phone rang. He answered, in case it was a business call for his dad. Wade had just started to say "Sterling residence" when a woman's frantic voice cut him off.

"Wynn, this is Violet," she said in a nasal twang.

"I'm not Wynn. I'm—" was all he could get out before she interrupted him.

"Wynn, don't lie to me. I recognize your voice.

You listen to me." Wade could hear the desperation in her tone as her words poured out louder and faster. "Your cell number has changed and I couldn't find you. Don't you dare hang up. We have a deal. You've been good about sending money, but it hasn't come this month. I need it, so get it to me. I'll keep my part of our bargain as long as you keep your promise and the money comes. I've stayed out of Dallas and no one knows about our child. If you want it to stay that way, get the money to me."

Shocked, Wade forgot about telling her who he was.

"It's in the mail, Violet," he said instead and hung up. He had given an answer and cut her off in the manner that Wynn would have done. She might learn Wynn had a twin and she had talked to the wrong brother, but he didn't think she would tell Wynn because she had given away his secret—Wynn had a child.

Stunned, Wade could imagine Wynn trying to hide the mother and the baby. Wynn's tastes ran to gorgeous, sexy women, but he didn't care if they were strippers in the worst nightclub in town or the cream of Dallas society. He always found the sexy beauties, but some of them he never took to meet the family. Violet, for one, he assumed.

He wondered about his folks not knowing their first grandchild. It might be just as well, and Wynn was paying regularly to bury the secret. He assumed Wynn had good reason to keep his baby a secret, so Wade would also, but it hurt to think there was a child out there that they'd never know and who would never know them.

He knew when his brother finally got around to marrying, it would be a dazzling beauty from a prominent, wealthy family. Someone like Olivia. Olivia would be a good match for Wynn because she could hold her own with him. Strong and bright, she would be a good influence on him.

For now, Wade would keep Wynn's secret. Wynn was a dad—that alone was an incredible shock. Another shiver ran down his spine. He couldn't imagine Wynn raising a child. He was still a child himself in many ways. But now he was a dad who probably had never even seen his own child. That wouldn't surprise Wade at all.

Wade thought about his own situation. He didn't want marriage or fatherhood at this point in his life, yet if he had a baby with a woman, he would want that child in his life. For just a moment he felt a pang and wondered if he would miss out on a lot by avoiding marriage. Then he had to laugh at himself. He didn't even have a woman in his life, since he was about to part ways with Olivia.

He kept his eyes on the road and pressed on the accelerator, trying to beat out the pending storm. But he couldn't outpace his thoughts. There was another problem, far more worrisome, on his mind. A few months ago his ranch foreman, Cotton Daniels, had told him that one of the cowboys was regularly receiving money from a man who drove to the ranch. Cotton happened to be taking out cedar trees when he saw the cowboy, Denny White, drive on a ranch road while a car came from the opposite direction and they parked facing each other. They didn't see Cotton because he was in a thick stand of cedars and his four-wheeler was out of the way. Initially he'd just passed it off as a gambling debt or some such, except the men were acting so secretive. The next month, about the same time, he saw them again near the gate.

Wade couldn't help but worry why someone was paying Denny.

Nor could he stop thinking this was another of the sneaky things Wynn was involved in. Wade had learned years earlier, if trouble occurred in his life, his twin was usually involved.

Throughout his life, Wade had never understood his twin's jealousy or his anger if Wade got something and he didn't. Wynn was their mother's favorite of her four children and he made certain he stayed that way. She was the one person on Earth that Wynn seemed to care about and went out of his way to keep happy.

Wade shook his head and sighed. When he got back to Dallas, he was going to have to deal with Wynn. He doubted if Wynn had delt with Denny face-to-face, but he felt certain that Wynn was behind whatever Denny was getting paid to do. Now he had to worry about that as well as Wynn's baby. His twin needed to tell the truth about his child. And he would have to wring out of Wynn if and what he was paying Denny to do. In the meantime he needed to give Cotton authority to fire Denny if he saw good reason. He trusted Cotton's judgment completely.

A clap of thunder brought Wade's attention back to his surroundings. The thunder rumbled ever closer.

The bumpy county road had mesquite scattered on either side. To his left was a deep canyon with a creek at the bottom. It was a small stream, but in a storm, Wade knew how streams could become white-water rivers and flood the surrounding area. He didn't want to get caught in a storm on a back road that was unknown terrain.

He hadn't seen another vehicle since he left the coast. He didn't have to worry about traffic, so he sped up, hoping to get to the next town before the storm hit. In minutes, the first big drops splashed on the windshield and then a gray sheet of blinding, torrential rain swept over his pickup.

Once, when he glanced in his rearview mirror at the sprays of water going up in his pickup's wake, he thought he saw headlights in the distance behind him. The rain was too intense to be sure. He soon swooshed around a curve and a sea of water was in front of him. As the road dipped, he pumped his brakes, but it was too late to prevent driving into the water rushing over the road, and then he felt the pickup leave the road and he was floating, swept up by the water.

Frantically, Wade yanked off his coat. If he went into the water at the bottom of the canyon and had to swim, he didn't want to be wearing a coat.

As thunder boomed and the first drops of rain fell, Ava Carter saw a pickup in the distance ahead. The drops turned into torrential rain and she could barely see anything except red taillights. Frowning, she pressed the accelerator, trying to narrow the distance. She rarely saw anyone on this back road in the area where she owned a cabin for an escape from her busy life in Dallas. She had been in Persimmon, the nearest small town, and had attempted to beat the storm back to her cabin, but she wasn't going to do it.

In Persimmon, when she'd heard that the weatherman had updated his forecast for torrential rains, she'd grabbed what supplies she could and left for her cabin.

It had surprised her to see taillights ahead on the usually deserted back road. If that was a stranger, someone unfamiliar with the area, the driver needed to turn around, too, because in a downpour the road would be under water in minutes.

She wanted to catch up enough to flag the driver, but the rain was too intense.

A deluge of rain hid the pickup's taillights from her view. She leaned on her horn, hoping that might make the person stop, but the rain and thunder probably drowned out the sound. Seconds later, she knew it was too late when the pickup vanished as the road turned in a sweeping curve. At that moment, another bolt of lightning illuminated the entire area and she saw water gush over the highway and the pickup wash off the road. As it went over the edge, still carried by the stream of water, a man jumped from the pickup, hit the ground and rolled down the incline, disappearing from her view. Carried by the rushing stream of water, the pickup crashed into a tree and was then swept around it, continuing down toward the raging creek.

Frightened for the man who jumped, she felt compelled to help him.

Ava pulled to the side of the road, leaving her lights blinking, even though she was certain no one else would happen along. She couldn't drive away and leave someone lying on the steep slope to the creek in this terrible storm, which was predicted to get worse.

She jammed on a broad-brimmed Resistol hat and yanked on a rain slicker. With a deep breath, she stepped out and ran to the edge of the road, where she looked for the driver. Rain made it difficult to spot anyone, so she cautiously started down the slope that was becoming slippery and muddy where there weren't weeds and high grass. Then she spotted the man sprawled on the ground, his fall evidently stopped by the low-lying branches of a cedar.

Soaked and chilled, she inched down the treacherous, steep slope. When she reached him, the stranger was lying still. As she thought about what to do, she kneeled beside him. To her relief, he stirred.

"Thank heavens, you're conscious," she said. Because of a blow to his head, a knot had popped out high on his brow at his hairline and his skin was already bruising. A deep cut across his shoulder bled even as rain washed over it. He didn't have a jacket, just a torn shirt, jeans and boots.

Cold rain pounded them and nearby a tree crashed to earth, taking small trees with it and leaving thick roots sticking up in the air, reminding her to hurry.

"We need to get back to the road to my pickup." She took his wrist to feel his pulse, which was strong. Then she reached out and pushed the tangled black hair off his face. When she brushed his face, his eyelids fluttered and she looked into brown eyes that suddenly held her attention as much as if he had reached out and touched her. Her gaze locked with his, caught and held as if in a trap. In spite of the raging storm, the world closed down to just the two of them. Her awareness of him rocked her and she could only stare at him, stunned.

She shouldn't be feeling anything except the cold, drenching rain. Since her broken engagement to Judd Porter, she had been numb to men, not wanting to go out with any of them. Not even her male friends. Being around any man brought back the painful memories of Judd. So how, then, could this total stranger, with chilling rain pouring over both of them in a raging storm, captivate her and make her heart race?

A clap of thunder and then a sizzling lightning bolt brought her out of the brief daze and she realized every second they were out in the storm, their situation grew worse.

As if he, too, sensed the danger, the man sat up and she was relieved to see he could move.

"You're sitting, so how's your back?"

He shrugged and grimaced. "My back is okay. My head feels as if someone is pounding it with a hammer."

"We need to get to my pickup. If I help you, can

you get up? And do you think you can make it back up this hill?"

"Yes, I can," he said as if there was no question about it.

"I have a cabin nearby. We have to get out of here before we get cut off by rising water. We can't go back to the last town now. Trees are falling and there's lightning. You're on an isolated back road. An ambulance wouldn't get here for an hour at best, and if the rain keeps up, an ambulance can't get here at all. I doubt if we can even get phone reception here. We can still drive to my cabin, I think." The whole time she talked, he gazed at her with such an intent look that her tingling response to him continued.

"Your cabin it is. Let's get out of here if you know a way."

"I do. It's not good, but it'll do. The weather predictions are getting worse."

"I'm ready," he said, standing without difficulty, and she realized he was fit and in good physical condition. She also noticed that he was tall, broad-shouldered and rather good-looking.

"Let me help you up the incline," she said, stepping beside him.

"I'll be okay," he said, as she thought he would. His shirt was ripped where he had fallen and been cut, the tattered, soaked material clinging to a muscled chest and a torn sleeve revealing a strong bicep.

"You'll have to look for your pickup later," she said.

"At the moment, that's not my worry."

"No, it isn't. We need to get to solid ground before

some of this incline gives way and takes us down with it," she said. "Let's go."

The climb was slippery, mud constantly making them lose their footing as they gradually neared the road.

Seconds later, there was a crack of tree limbs breaking and then another tall oak fell. He pushed her away from the tree and not even the tips of leaves touched them, but chunks of ground broke off and slid downhill.

She slipped and he stepped close to put his arm around her as she grabbed him. "Thanks. I'm glad that wasn't your cut shoulder," she said, holding her hat on her head as she looked up at him.

As they steadied, he gripped a tree branch with one hand while he held her close with the other, her hip pressed against him. She gazed at him. Wind battered them and a sheet of cold rain swept over them, but she barely noticed it. Even with his injuries, he was strong, holding her tightly while his body heat warmed her side where they were pressed together.

As she gazed into his brown eyes, another sizzle made her forget rain, cold, danger—everything else except his strong arm holding her, his warm body against hers and those eyes that captured and held her gaze. Dark brown eyes that changed her world. When she saw the slightest narrowing of his eyes, she knew he felt something, too. She figured this primitive urge they both had was stirred by the danger from the storm. As if to confirm her thoughts, another big tree snapped and cracked, toppling to the ground.

"Let's get out of here," she shouted with a deliberate effort to break the spell. His arm tightened around her waist and, together, grabbing nearby limbs, they climbed the remaining way to the road. She pointed to her pickup. "You wait here and I'll come get you."

With a shake of his head, he took her arm and started toward her pickup. "Let's go."

When they reached her vehicle, he released her. As soon as they both were inside, she retrieved a first-aid kit from the back seat and handed him a thick gauze pad.

"Hold this against your shoulder. You're still losing blood."

He took the pad from her and placed it over the jagged cut on his shoulder. As he did, he reached out to remove her hat and toss it into the back, then he turned to take a long, slow look at her that made her forget she was cold and rain-soaked. All she knew was that his attention was on her and she couldn't get her breath.

"When I opened my eyes, you looked like an angel with your blond hair and blue eyes, but I don't think angels wear cowboy hats."

His voice was deep and he sat close while his dark brown eyes made her heart race. He had raked thick, wet black hair away from his face, but a few wavy locks had already slipped free to fall on his forehead. Regardless of his injuries and tattered, wet clothes, she felt another puzzling moment of heated, physical awareness. How could she feel intense awareness for a total stranger, and in these abominable circumstances?

She made an effort to break the eye contact and get

her mind back on their situation, which grew more hazardous by the minute.

She cleared her throat and dug out her phone. "I'll try to get info on the roads," she said with a breathlessness that she hoped he didn't notice. She focused on her phone for a moment and then shook her head and dropped her phone into a pocket of her jacket when she got no reception.

"My cabin is big, well-stocked and comfortable," she said, starting the pickup and driving back the way she had come. "We'll have to double back for a few miles to get there. If this downpour continues a lot longer, we may be stuck at my place until the storm is gone and water recedes. It's remote and isolated out here. As you can see, there's no cell-phone reception. No TV reception, either, so I don't even have a TV at the cabin."

"How many miles to your cabin?"

"About ten. There's a road I can take and it's on higher ground. It's a back road the ranchers put in across private property, but it gives about five of us a way around the low places when we have these torrential downpours. There are two bad things about the road—it's gravel and we have one creek to cross," she said as they continued on.

"A gravel road is okay. I remember a narrow road and a sign—'Keep Off. Private Property.'"

"That's it." She glanced at him because she noticed he was shifting and patting his pockets as he talked. "Is something wrong?"

Frowning, he looked at her. "I don't have my wallet. I must have lost it rolling down the hill. We can't go searching for it now," he said.

"No, we can't."

"No telling where my pickup has gone."

"There's no finding that now, either," she said, concentrating on her driving in the downpour. Thunder was loud and lightning lit up the area. "We need to get to my cabin before we're cut off from any shelter. There aren't many people who live out here."

"So I noticed."

"Yes, and it's not a good place to be in a storm like this. From here to the gravel road will take about five more minutes and then it'll be even slower traveling. We have one more bridge to cross." Her brow creased as a thought occurred to her. "If we can't get across that, I don't think we can get back to Persimmon. I'm sure the old bridge to Persimmon is under water by now." She shrugged it off. "Not to worry. If we can cross that last bridge, my cabin is on high ground. It's never flooded."

As she squinted through the rain-soaked windshield, she told him, "The road we're on is such a back road, it's seldom used even by those of us who live in this area. I have a close neighbor and we could go to his house, but he's nearer to the creek and that's probably already like a raging river. I wouldn't feel safe in his house in this storm."

She glanced at him. "How are you feeling?"

"My head is pounding, my shoulder still hurts and I'm thoroughly soaked. Otherwise, fair to middlin', I'd say. Thank you again for stopping to pick me up."

"Sure."

He didn't say anything else and she thought he might be tired of conversation and hurting. "Don't go to sleep in case you have a concussion."

"I don't think staying awake will be a problem," he remarked dryly and she wondered how much pain he was in. Or perhaps he was worrying about having lost his wallet and his pickup, which she suspected was downstream somewhere filled with water or smashed on rocks.

"I don't have my phone, either," he said.

"You can't use it out here, anyway." For a moment she was quiet. "I think it's time we get introduced. I'm Ava Carter."

"I'm glad to meet you, Ava Carter," he said in a somber tone of voice.

They rode in silence and she wondered why he didn't introduce himself. When she glanced at him, he had such a worried expression on his face, she put her foot on the brake and turned to him. "What's wrong?"

"You don't know me at all, yet you know something is wrong."

She nodded. "You look concerned. Should I be worried about your identity?"

Shaking his head, he answered, "Well, yes and no, I don't think so. But that's just a feeling I have, because the problem is—" he hesitated only a moment as he stared at her "—I can't tell you my name. I don't know it. I can't remember who I am or where I'm from."

# Two

She stared at him. "Maybe we should turn around and try to get to a hospital."

She grabbed her phone. "I'll try again to get through." But after a moment she put it away. "I can't get any reception. We're out of range." She debated what to do. He would get better professional care in a hospital, but she was certain the roads would already be closed. Sheets of rain still swept over them and wind shook her pickup. "I feel sure by now the roads to the nearest hospital are closed. Even if we could go back, Persimmon doesn't have a hospital."

"Does it have a doctor?"

"They have a vet and people go to him. But my close neighbor is a nurse. That sounds like the best we can do."

"Sounds good to me. Let's go to your cabin…unless you're concerned about my identity. I don't think I'm dangerous."

She looked into his dark brown eyes and he gazed back at her. She couldn't understand her reasoning, but she felt okay about him. She hoped her judgment was sound. But then again, she didn't really have much choice. She wasn't going to leave him out in this storm to survive on his own.

Her gaze drifted over him, noticing again his expensive watch. His boots were covered with mud, but she could see part of them, as well as his belt, which looked hand-tooled and expensive. All meaningless as far as judging his character, however.

She shook her head and smiled. "I don't think so, either, although I trust you for reasons I don't understand. It's just that I feel a connection with you. Do you know what state you're in?"

"Texas. I saw the tag on your pickup so we can't make any judgments from that answer."

"Maybe not, but you gave me an honest answer. Do you know where you live?"

He frowned briefly and then shook his head. "Nothing comes to me. I have glimmers of things, but I don't know if they're from real life, television or friends of mine. I'm at a loss. I don't recall my parents, my friends, or where I live. Or what commitments I have."

"We'll assume you have some kind of family—parents, siblings."

"I don't have a wedding ring," he said as he looked

down at his left hand. Then he turned his gaze back to her, shaking his head. "If my phone and wallet with all my info were in my pickup and it went into that stream, there's no telling if it'll be found, or by whom. Or maybe they fell out of my pockets when I slid down that slope. In all that mud and the rain, they may never be found."

He looked dazed and dejected, and thoroughly confused, and she felt the need to bolster him. "We'll deal with that later. Right now, let's talk." When he looked at her quizzically, she added, "You've had a head injury so you need to stay awake, and one way for me to know you're awake is for you to talk."

"We can both talk," he said. "Are you a rancher? Or in a rancher's family?" he asked her.

"No to both. I'm an occupational therapist and I have my own home-care business in Dallas. I provide caregivers. It's busy and sometimes I want to get away. I have someone who works for me who can take over when I come stay at my cabin. I did own a ranch that I inherited from my grandfather. I sold it to Gerald Roan, who lives on it. His wife, Molly, is the nurse I mentioned. I kept five acres—it's where my cabin is. I have three horses and a few head of cattle that Gerald takes care of. I wanted a cabin away from Dallas where it's quiet, in the great outdoors and there's a horse I can ride and a place to ride it."

She turned on the gravel road, slowing to a crawl. "Here's our private road." The road was rough and the rain was still a blinding downpour.

"This is a roundabout way to get home, but we

only cross one creek and it has a strong bridge that hopefully will be above water. I've only seen it underwater once before, but this is a bad storm."

While she concentrated on her driving, he was silent. Night was approaching and she wanted to get to her cabin and out of the downpour before dark. With the storm it would get dark earlier than usual. After a few minutes, she stopped to try her phone again.

"There's a stretch here of fairly open country that's the highest point in the area, where I can sometimes get service. I want to try again to contact Gerald. He's got a four-story house on a hill, so that gives him a higher place to send and receive messages. At least his equipment works better than at my place, where I can't get any reception at all in this kind of weather."

She tried calling Gerald but got nowhere. Then she tried texting him. "Also, I'll try to text the sheriff in Persimmon to let him know about you in case he gets a missing-person's report." In minutes she shook her head. "I can't get through to the sheriff. I don't know if it's the distance or the direction or what. I did send a text to my neighbor and it went through, I think, but he hasn't answered." She was suddenly tense about going home with a stranger who didn't know his own identity. Worse, if the bridge was underwater, they would be trapped outside for a night in the car. She didn't want to think about that one at all.

In minutes, she got a text in return and Gerald offered to come stay if she was concerned and asked about the man's identity.

She sent another brief text to Gerald that the

stranger had received a blow to his head and he couldn't remember his identity. Also, she relayed that his wallet and phone were missing.

Gerald wrote that he would drop by and she sent her thanks. She regretted that Gerald had to go out in the storm, but felt better about taking in a stranger who said he didn't remember anything about his identity and he didn't have any ID. Judging from the knot on his head, she felt he was telling the truth, but she was glad Gerald would come meet him. She drove forward.

"So what did your neighbor have to say?" he asked her a few moments later.

"I told him about bringing you home with me and he wrote back that he's coming by to meet you."

She glanced at the stranger and he smiled—a smile that made her heart skip beats. Another unwanted reaction, now more than ever. She didn't want to respond to any man right now, not when she was still getting over a broken heart, and definitely not one who had no memory of himself.

"It could make life easier temporarily if I take an assumed name just so you can get my attention or introduce me or whatever we have to do," he said.

"Of course. You're right. Pick a name you like."

"Bill Smith is easy," he said after a moment. "That sounds okay. It would be funny if it turned out to be my real name and that's why it sounds okay," he said and smiled again—another smile that made her heart skip a beat. She tried to ignore her reaction, but that wasn't easy.

"Okay, Bill it is. That's a good name," she said. They started downhill and she kept her attention on the road. "There goes the last time I can hope to get a text through. I'll always try if I need to send one, but from here on, I'm cut off from the world except for the people who live around me. Gerald and his family are close neighbors. The people who work for Gerald live on his property. Some of those people work for me, too." Concern for keeping him awake took a back seat as they approached the creek she had to cross. As she drew close, she gasped and slowed to a crawl.

"That's Blue Creek," she said. "I've only seen it like this once before. It's usually ankle-deep, but it's a river now. The bridge is supposed to be well-built and the water isn't totally over it yet," she observed, watching waves splash against the bridge. "I'm going to try to cross it. Otherwise we'll have to stay out here in my pickup all night. That's not a good alternative."

"If the bridge is as sturdy and well-built as you say, we should be able to cross without trouble." He unfastened his seatbelt. "Unbuckle. You don't want to be buckled in if the bridge collapses."

She unbuckled her seatbelt and drove cautiously, praying the bridge would stand. Holding her breath, she started across.

"You're doing fine," he said. "Nothing is shaking and that's a good sign. Not much farther," he added as they inched across. "Doing good. Across!" he announced, turning to give her a high five as he flashed a big smile. "Good job."

His irresistible smile sent a tingle to her toes while

her heartbeat quickened. At the same time, every positive response she had to him stirred another instant negative response in a reminder that she should squelch any attraction she felt. She didn't want to be tempted by a man who made her heart race by just a smile. Especially a man who couldn't recall his own name.

The attraction felt more dangerous and a bigger threat to her well-being than the raging storm and rising water, which didn't make sense to her, but was true just the same.

She drove a few feet away from the bridge and paused to buckle her seatbelt again while he fastened his. "We're on this side now and there's no going back. That bridge will be underwater in minutes," she said. "Good news is we're close to my cabin with no more creeks or rivers to cross. Bad news is, with no reception, if your family starts looking for you and puts your picture on television or social media, we'll never know it until this storm is over and I can get to town or far enough back down the road."

"We can't do anything about that now."

He was right. "In addition to the tornado threat, Gerald mentioned that the storm has intensified."

As if to underscore her words about the storm, thunder boomed and a streak of lightning struck a tree, traveling down the trunk, splitting it in two and running a few feet along the ground as both parts of the tree crashed to earth. Knowing they needed to get to shelter, she continued driving.

They rode in silence until she turned on a paved

drive. When she slowed in front of large black iron fencing, big gates swung open to let her enter. She glanced at him again. "You're getting a black eye below that bump on your forehead. Actually, the bump has gone down."

"That's good."

The gates closed behind her as she drove on. "Well, we made it to my place," she said.

"Yes, we did. You might have saved my life today, you know," he said in a solemn voice.

Startled, she glanced at him. "I think you would have survived if I hadn't been driving past. You seem strong and healthy. You got up to the road without any difficulty."

"I'm damn glad you came back to get me and I'm not out in this weather without a car or wallet or memory." He dipped his head and looked out the window. "AC Ranch," he said, reading.

"It's not really a ranch any longer since I sold it. I kept the AC Ranch sign because Gerald didn't care. He renamed his ranch Roan Ranch."

Though the rain was still steady, the lightning and thunder had diminished. They followed the winding road that ran between mesquite, all leaning to the north because of the prevailing winds, and then a few stretches of open space.

After going around a curve, they topped a slight rise and she waved one hand. "You can't see much for the rain, but there's my cabin. If you can make it out, you can see there's plenty of room for a guest."

"What I can see is not exactly a little log cabin.

How many bedrooms do you have?" he asked, sounding amused.

"Six bedrooms—three are suites—and seven bathrooms. I don't have family now, but I do have friends and this is usually a relaxing getaway. There's a gym, too. I'll show you around."

"You're a long ways from a town. You take care of all this yourself?"

She smiled and shook her head. "Thank heavens, no. It's easy to hire help of all sorts from Gerald's ranch. Like I said, his house and buildings are close to my property."

"That's a good setup. But calling it a cabin doesn't exactly convey an accurate image of your getaway home," he remarked dryly.

She smiled. "True. But I love it here. My dream has always been to marry and have four or five kids to fill it."

He laughed and shook his head. "I don't have any idea, but I seriously doubt if I've ever taken out a woman whose lifelong wish was for marriage and four or five kids."

"Well, when you get your memory back, you might be surprised. I can say this, though—you probably have never taken out anyone who had no family."

"No family?"

She shook her head. "I don't have any family left. My mom and sister died from cancer. My dad moved away and remarried. My grandparents aren't alive." She shrugged. "So, essentially, I'm alone." When she saw his mood start to sag, she added, "But I'm okay with it. My work and friends keep me plenty busy."

"You said you're an occupational therapist with a home-care business in Dallas. It must be a booming business."

"We're busy, which is good. I have a much simpler place in Dallas, but I love this cabin and I built it for my future, for my dream home. Right now it's a vacation home, a getaway, so I don't have a landline or Wi-Fi. Just peace and quiet." She looked at the cabin and envisioned it without the torrents of rain marring its beauty. "Luckily I had this home when my mom and sister could still come out here to visit, before I lost my family. I'll bet you have siblings."

"I wish I could remember even one thing about my family."

"A family is wonderful. My sister was ten years older, so when I was growing up, she wasn't around. I love children and I love kids and I'm thinking about someday going back to night classes or taking online courses to get a teacher's certificate. I have a master's in occupational therapy. All I would need for secondary teaching would be the required education courses and student teaching. It's not a whole lot. Either that or I'll just volunteer for things that involve kids. Now I'm doing something that helps people, so I'm not ready to give up the home-care business yet. It's work I like."

He studied her with a thoughtful look and she wondered what he was thinking. He turned away.

"That's commendable—helping people. I can't remember what the hell I do," he said.

"You'll remember eventually."

"Thanks again for coming to my rescue, Ava. I know you'd feel better if I could tell you who I am and what I do. Being friendly and grateful to be rescued aren't necessarily guarantees of a good guy," he remarked dryly. "With you being isolated out here—"

She cut him off. "I'm not really isolated here because of Gerald and his wife, the cowboys who work at Roan Ranch and their families, some of whom work for me. And Samantha cooks for me, although she's off right now because her daughter had a baby. Samantha is married to one of Gerald's cowboys. The wife of one of the cowhands, Margo, cleans, and Jonah and his crew do the yard work for me and for the Roans. I have people around all the time. Margo won't be here until next week because she was here yesterday. Oh, this is the first Monday in October in case you're interested."

"Neither the month or day means much to me right now. I don't know where I was going or where I had been. I don't know why I was where I was." He blew out a frustrated breath and raked a hand through his hair. When he turned to her again, he changed the subject. "You said your father remarried. Do you see him?"

"No, I don't. He divorced my mom when I was fourteen. He and his new wife live in California. I don't see him at all. They severed relations and he doesn't contact me."

Though it was sad that her father wasn't part of her life, she didn't feel sorry for herself. She had lots of good memories of growing up with both her parents. Which was more than this man sitting beside her could say right now.

She continued up the drive and turned off the main road that circled in front of the house. She took a branch road that veered around the house to a porte cochere along the west side.

"We're home," she said cheerfully as she put the vehicle in Park. Then she turned to see his reaction to the cabin up close, only to find him instead looking intently at her. Her eyes met his and suddenly it became another moment when she was conscious of him as a physically appealing male. She didn't know anything about him and she was about to take him in and let him stay at her house, under her roof, with her. And that thought made her heart race, but not with fear.

Breaking the spell that seemed to have fallen over her, a bright red pickup pulled in beside them and she smiled when she saw it was Gerald and Molly.

"Here are the Roans minus their kids. They have a sitter for them easily available—Gerald's grandmother lives on his ranch. Her house is close to Gerald's."

"It's weird to meet someone when you don't even know who you are," he remarked as he stepped out.

Even though they had both parked beneath a roof and were sheltered, the wind and torrential rain still blew through the porte cochere and Ava motioned for everyone to follow as she went ahead, opened the door and entered her house. The Roans were both bringing boxes and covered dishes as they hurried inside and set their packages on the floor so they could take off their wet coats.

As soon as they were inside the dark entryway with a terrazzo floor, she turned to face the Roans. "Let me help you get these wet coats off," Ava insisted. She turned to flip a switch.

"First, we don't have electric power because of the storm," Ava said, getting a flashlight from a shelf by the door. "I'll turn on the generators, but before I go, let me make the introductions," she said as she took off her rain slicker and hung it on a hook. When she turned, she noticed the stranger's gaze sweep over her and instantly she became aware of her tangled, long blond hair, her blue sweater and dark jeans. His gaze reached her toes and then went back up to meet her eyes, and she could feel the heat in her cheeks as they looked at each other.

To her relief, Molly was talking about dinner and Gerald had just finished hanging up their yellow slickers and hats, and he seemed distracted as he picked up boxes he was carrying when he came.

"We're calling him Bill Smith until his memory returns," she said to the Roans as she passed small flashlights to everyone.

"Bill, meet my neighbors. This is Gerald Roan," she said as Gerald balanced two big boxes he carried, stuck out his hand and they shook. Gerald was almost as tall as the stranger.

"Meet my wife, Molly," Gerald said easily, turning to his brunette wife, who only came to Gerald's shoulder in height. As always, she had a warm smile and Ava was once again thankful for them as neighbors. Molly held a stack of three covered bowls in her hands.

"Thanks for coming by," Bill said.

"I'm close and this is easy," Gerald answered, shaking out the rain. "Here's some clothes I don't want back," he said to Bill, indicating the top box he held. "I thought you might need something dry."

"Thank you," Bill replied, taking the box from him and placing it on the floor of the entryway. "That's good because all I have is what I'm wearing and this shirt is all ripped."

"Bill," Ava said, "I told you Molly was a nurse, so you might let her look at your injuries."

Smiling, Molly held up the bowls and a black bag dangled from her right arm. "I carry this for emergencies. I can look at your cuts. We have two kids, so I constantly practice my nursing skills."

"Thanks," he said, "to both of you." He nodded to Molly, then turned to Ava and flashed another one of those smiles that made her pulse jump. She glanced at Gerald and was relieved he hadn't been looking at her. She hoped her tingling responses to the stranger didn't show.

"Also, we brought dinner in case you two haven't eaten," Molly said, indicating the bowls. "We had a fish fry today and it was easy to bring some. I'll put all this in the refrigerator."

"Thank you so much," Ava said, smiling at Molly.

"It smells wonderful. I'll admit, I haven't given a thought to eating or even asked if you had lunch today," she said, turning to the stranger, finding it difficult to think of him as Bill Smith. "I'll get the generators turned on and we can see what we're doing."

"I'll go with you," Gerald said. "This box goes to the kitchen," he said to Bill as he handed him the other box. "I know where your generators are and I can help," he said, and went off with Ava.

After getting the generators going, they walked back into the entryway. When they did, Ava and Gerald joined them.

"We put the food away," Ava said. "It's good to have lights again."

"Now that we have lights, before Molly looks at my cuts, I need to wash the mud off." The stranger turned to Ava. "I'd like a shower more than anything, if that's okay. It won't take me long."

"Go shower and when you're dressed, if you'll call me, I'll come tend to those cuts," Molly said easily.

"Gerald, you and Molly make yourself comfortable in the family room," Ava said. "I'll show Bill where he can shower." She turned to him. "Come with me."

"Gladly," he said. "I feel covered in mud, sticks and leaves." He looked at Gerald and paused. "Is there something you wanted to say to me?"

Gerald shook his head. "No. Sorry if I'm staring, but you look familiar."

"That's good news," Bill Smith said with relief in his voice. "If you recognize me or recall meeting me, that would give a clue to my identity. Whether it's good or bad, I'd welcome knowing because not knowing who I am and not remembering anything from my past is not a good feeling. Losing my wallet didn't help. It didn't occur to me to hang on to it even at a risk to my life."

"I might be wrong, but I think I've seen you before or met you. I hope it comes to me," Gerald said. "I promise to tell you if it does."

"Thanks." Bill picked up the box of clothes and turned to follow Ava down a wide hall.

"I hope to hell he remembers and does know me or at least recognizes me, even if it was a 'Wanted' poster," he said and she smiled.

"You're wearing jeans, boots, a Western-style shirt. Gerald lives and breathes ranching. I'm guessing you're a Texas rancher and you've crossed paths before. Underneath that black hair that falls on your forehead, you have a pale strip of forehead while the rest of your face is tan. That pale strip indicates you've spent time outside and you were wearing a hat."

She stopped to take his free hand in hers and turn his hand over. As she ran her finger lightly over his palm, she noticed two things—his calluses and her reaction to touching him. Immediately she released his hand and started walking again.

"Whoever you are, you have calluses that indicate that you work with your hands. A lot of ranchers have calluses." She tried for nonchalance, but there was no denying she felt anything but. When she'd taken

his hand she had been thinking only about his identity. The moment her fingers had wrapped around
his warm hand, her physical awareness of him had
intensified and she knew for both their sakes, she
shouldn't have touched him.

"Want to look at my hand again and see what else
comes to you?" he asked in a huskier tone of voice.

Startled, she looked up at him and realized he was
teasing, actually flirting with her and she wondered
whether it was because he was aware of those same
sparks when they touched.

Smiling, she shook her head. "I think we better
leave well enough alone when you know nothing
about yourself."

"I know a few things about myself that I've realized since you showed up to rescue me," he drawled
in a deeper voice that sent tingles up her spine and
heightened her awareness of him.

"You're hurt, have amnesia, you're with total
strangers...and you're flirting." Smiling, she shook
her head. "You must be feeling better."

"I think you're causing the way I feel, and believe
me, it's a dang big improvement over what's been
happening."

She laughed. "You better cool it until you learn
who you are."

"I don't think I can be held responsible for any innocent remarks I make right now when I don't even
know who I am."

"They aren't so innocent and you know enough

to realize what you're saying," she said, laughing at him and he grinned.

"Meeting you has been worth going through all that happened to me. At least, sort of, because I do want my memory to return."

"Cool it, cowboy. And I think I'm right—you're a rancher."

She turned into a room. "I'm down the hall but here's a guest suite you can use," she said as they entered a living area. Through an open door she could see the bedroom that had a blue-and-tan decor, like the sitting room. "You'll find packets of things you might need—comb, soap, toothbrush, that sort of thing—in the bathroom. There should be clean towels, too. There will be about two sizes of new pajamas on one of the chests. I'm glad Gerald brought you some men's clothes. On second thought, let me check to make sure the soap is there," she said, starting to turn away.

He stopped her with his words. "Go join your friends," he said. "I'm sure I'll have what I need. You sound as well-equipped as a drugstore. At least, I can remember what a drugstore is."

Before she could step away, he reached out to take her arm. The moment he touched her, she felt another tingle all the way to her toes. Her breath caught and she looked up to meet his gaze that was as sizzling as his light touch on her arm. Startled, she saw he felt something, too. He had a surprised look that changed to an intense focus on her, which made her pulse drum faster.

She should say something, move, do something, but she felt captured by a casual touch and a look. Only the touch hadn't been casual to her and it evidently hadn't been to him.

"Call me if you need me. It's Ava, in case you forgot," she said in a breathless voice that was almost a whisper.

"I can't remember my name, but I promise you, I remember yours, Ava," he said in a husky voice, still gazing at her with a curious look that kept her pulse racing. He released her arm and, with an effort, she turned to leave.

She hurried out, closing the door to his suite behind her. She stood a moment and gulped for air. She had never had such a reaction to a man. Never, not once. How could a casual, slight touch stir such desire? Especially by a muddy man who was a complete stranger?

After her breakup she hadn't been attracted to any man. She had turned down invitations, not wanting to date. She still didn't want to.

She was shocked by her reaction to this man. Especially now. Her heartbreak over Judd definitely had not healed and would never be forgotten. It still hurt to think about how he'd left her.

At this point in her life she didn't want to be attracted to any man. She couldn't handle another breakup.

So how could just a look from this stranger make her heart race?

He'd seemed as surprised as she was and she was

certain it was every bit as unwanted a reaction to him as it was to her.

Telling herself to stop thinking about him, she hurried back to join her neighbors and thank Molly for bringing her nurse kit to tend to the stranger's cuts. Ava was relieved that she wouldn't have to do that task. The mere thought of taking care of his back or shoulder, or any other part of his anatomy where he had been injured, made her pulse race again. She banished the thought as she rejoined her friends.

"You're the greatest neighbors to go out in this storm to come by and meet him, in addition to bringing food, clothing and first-aid care. Thank you both."

"We're glad to do it," Molly said.

"I feel better meeting him," Gerald added. "I can't recall why he looks familiar, but I have a real strong feeling we've met before."

"That's good news, too," she said. "Right now he knows nothing about himself."

She looked out the window at the storm, which hadn't let up. "I hope your kids aren't afraid with both of you gone. That wind is fierce and the rain is still teeming." As if to emphasize her words, a streak of lightning lit the outside. Shortly, thunder boomed again and wind whistled around her house.

"The kids don't care. They're super good at entertaining themselves and, fortunately, both like to read, so they're either playing a game or curled up to read or comforting my grandmother over this storm," Gerald answered. "She's the one who will be scared out of her wits."

Thunder boomed and the sharp click of hail drowned out conversation for a moment. Gerald went to the window and then disappeared briefly. In a moment he returned. "Look at the size of this hail. This is slightly bigger than the other we had," he said, crossing the room to show them. "There will be roof and window damages with this storm."

Molly gasped, picking up a hailstone that looked the size of a golf ball.

"It's already let up," he said, taking the hailstones to the kitchen to toss them into the sink. "I think this storm will make the news," he said when he returned.

"Thank goodness the hail didn't last long," Ava said, looking at the window.

"Your dinner is in the fridge now," Molly reminded her. "And, of course, you know you both are always welcome at our house if you'd rather stay there."

"Thanks, Molly. I think we'll be fine."

She heard boot heels scrape the floor as Bill Smith walked into the room.

"I feel infinitely better after that shower," he said, entering the room, and Ava's pulse jumped. His hair was neatly combed. He wore jeans Gerald had furnished and his own boots, now with the mud scraped off and cleaned.

"Thanks again for the clothes, Gerald. I'm glad to get out of the others. Except for my shirt, which I threw into the trash, I brought my wet clothes with me in case I can throw them into a washer if you don't mind. I washed the mud off the clothes, so if you'll tell me where your washer is, I'll put these in."

He was bare-chested and he looked strong and fit with bulging muscles and tan skin. Thick black hair curled across the center of his chest. He still had the dark shadow of facial hair on his chin and jaw. She looked up to meet his gaze. Had he seen her looking so intently at him?

He held a hand towel pressed against his shoulder. "I'm sorry to bleed on your towel," he said to Ava and then turned to Molly. "If you want to look at my cuts, this is the time."

"Go into the kitchen near the sink," Ava said. "The light is good in there and you can pull a chair over or you can go back to his suite. It has a big bathroom."

"I know the way," Molly said, crossing the room. "C'mon. We'll put your clothes in to wash and then I'll see what I can do for you."

Ava watched the stranger leave the room. He had muscles, something else that might indicate ranch work. "I'm glad Molly's here to patch him up."

"If you're worried about staying here with him," Gerald said, "both of you can come stay at our house, like Molly said, or he can go home with us."

"I'll be okay."

"Once again, I honestly think I know him. It'll probably come to me in the middle of the night. With this storm and the area we're in, I won't be able to text or call you if I do remember, but if I know him, he's an okay guy. I don't know the other kind."

"A rancher seems likely. I saw his pickup when he jumped out of it. It was one of the big ones."

"I'll pick him up tomorrow and let him look at

my horses. If he's a rancher, the horses might jog his memory."

"That would be nice if it works out, but if we're still having storms, don't come out."

He grinned. "I wish my horses would tell me that," he said and she smiled.

Soon Molly and the stranger returned. It was difficult to think of him as Bill Smith because that really wasn't his name. Now he wore a long-sleeved blue denim shirt that Gerald had brought. His arms were slightly longer than Gerald's and his shoulders were broader, so the sleeves were short. He had the shirt tucked into his jeans and his shirt had the top three buttons undone. His injured shoulder was bandaged, with only a tiny part of the bandage showing. He was handsome and the sight of him, even with his blackened eye, forehead bump and bruises, still took her breath away.

"I feel better. Now if I just can remember who I am, life would be great." He turned to Molly. "Thanks for coming out in the storm to help and for tending to my wounds."

"Glad to do it," she said while Gerald put on his hat and coat and held out Molly's slicker for her while she slipped into it.

Bill turned to Gerald. "Thank you for bringing the clothes. I appreciate it. In this storm that's a big deal."

Gerald put his arm across Molly's shoulders. "I didn't want to wait for the rain to let up because from the predictions, we're supposed to have three big storms move through here. I think this is still storm number one." He turned to Ava. "We'll go, but if you want us for any reason, turn on your yard lights. We can see them and if it's late at night, turn them on and then step outside and fire three shots into the ground. The dogs will bark and all the ruckus will wake me. I'll hear them and come over."

"I think we'll be fine." She followed them out to their vehicle while her guest stayed behind in the house.

Molly turned to her. "I gave him instructions on things to do, take it easy, take care of himself. No alcohol. He shouldn't sleep right away. He has everything written so he can show you. Here's a short list for you," she said, giving Ava a torn piece of paper. "This isn't my area of expertise, but I think those are things he should do. He was interested and seems cooperative."

"Thank you so much for all you've done tonight. I wouldn't have known how to help him."

"You would have done okay," Molly said, smiling. "We better go."

Gerald paused once he opened the truck door. He looked back at Ava. "I meant what I said about firing some shots," he told her.

She smiled. "I don't think I'll need to do that. I think you're right about him being a rancher."

Gerald nodded. "I agree. I may remember who he is or at least where we met. We need to know and he needs to know."

She waited under the porte cochere until Gerald

drove into the storm and his taillights disappeared in the darkness and the rain.

When she went back inside, once again, it was just the two of them. Her and the stranger. She was confident that Gerald knew him and would eventually remember how and where, and she wasn't afraid to have him as a guest. She was far more afraid of her own reactions to him, of the unwanted, fiery attraction she felt that drew her to him, a connection that was pulling her in.

Her worry was, alone with him, could she resist his charm and sex appeal?

# Three

When she rejoined him in the large living area, he turned from the window and gave her a smile. And that's when Ava knew exactly how hard it would be to resist this man. Whoever he was.

"Ava, I can't thank you enough for coming back for me today. Not everybody would have done that." He walked toward her and his focus was intently on her eyes. "I'm very grateful."

Better he be grateful from a distance, she thought, sidestepping him and turning toward the kitchen. "No problem. How about that dinner now? Are you ready to eat?"

"That sounds great. Let me help."

Not only did she want her space, but she also remembered Molly's directions. "You should take it easy. I'll get everything on and you can sit and watch. Molly told me you shouldn't sleep right away and no alcohol. She gave me a list of foods good for you and, fortunately, what they had for dinner tonight is good for you—bass."

"Yeah, she told me when she worked on my shoulder that the bass is great." He flexed his shoulder a bit. "My shoulder doesn't bother me as much as my head and my memory loss. I hope she's right that the memory loss won't last." He followed Ava into the kitchen. "I can help you get things on the table, at least."

As she took dishes out of a cabinet, she said, "No way. You sit and watch." Only when she turned did she realize how close he had been standing behind her. She was caught again by those deep brown eyes as her gaze locked with his, and she was swamped by another moment of intense awareness. Another moment of desire. She should move, look away, do anything except what she was doing—standing immobile, barely able to breathe, her heart racing. But she felt trapped in his gaze. Her pulse drummed when she looked at his lips—he had a well-shaped mouth that took her breath away even more.

"I don't know why this happens." She thought she'd only said it to herself, until his eyes flared. "I—I think you should go sit across the room."

But he didn't move. He held his ground and held her gaze. "I don't know why this happens, either. But I'm your guest so I'll do what you want. But we may be missing something here by our restraint. After all," he said in a husky voice, "a kiss isn't a commitment. And this is a good night for a kiss."

His head lowered toward hers, but to keep him away, she placed a hand on his chest—a hard, muscled chest that did nothing to douse the desire that was burning inside her. "I think we should stick to restraint," she cautioned, making herself say the words. "We can't go wrong with restraint." She felt like she was lecturing herself instead of him. Her words were breathless. How could he ignite desire by just looking at her and standing close?

He paused a moment before he spoke. "Your call," he said, then turned and walked away. As he crossed to the table, she let out her breath. She watched him pull out a chair and sit to face her.

"I'll get dinner on," she said, aware her words were still spoken breathlessly. She was acutely conscious of his dark-eyed gaze following her as she got out dishes to set two places.

"I don't have any memory of my life. You, on the other hand, remember your life full well. So tell me about yourself. Is there a man in your life?"

"No, not at all."

"I find that difficult to imagine," he remarked dryly and she had to smile at him.

"I was engaged and we broke it off and I really haven't wanted to go out with anyone since that happened."

"May I ask why you broke the engagement?"

"Sure," she said, avoiding looking at him and trying to sound casual, busying herself with removing the containers from the fridge. "Actually, he broke the engagement to marry someone else. That was early last spring. I really haven't wanted to go out with anyone since then. That may change someday, but right now because I got hurt, I'm not ready for a relationship." She stopped to look at him and smiled. "Definitely not with anyone who doesn't know his identity. I'm sure you agree on that one."

"Oh, yeah—I don't want to have complicated my life in the meantime."

While the fish and vegetables reheated, she set a tossed green salad on the table, along with tall glasses of water for him and for herself.

His fingers closed around her wrist, stopping her and holding her near him. "This may not be the time to pursue it, but you can't deny there's something between us. Something that comes out of the blue. I won't forget it, Ava, and I know there may come a time to explore it a little."

She didn't deny it, knew she couldn't, not when he could feel her pulse jump and race as she looked down at him. "I've never had it happen with a complete stranger," she whispered and he flashed that smile that made her heart pound and made her want to step closer to him. "I better move away right now," she said breathlessly without moving an inch. He stood, putting him even closer to her. Mere inches were between them and his gaze held hers and stole her breath.

"Damn, I wasn't going to do this," he said in a husky whisper. "We both just agreed we wouldn't, but I can't resist when you get me wound up with just a look. I know full well you don't even want to have that effect."

"No, I don't," she whispered. They stared at each other. She couldn't move or look away.

"You don't want to step away any more than I want to. Just say to hell with it," he whispered and closed the last tiny bit of distance between them. He paused just long enough for her to put her arms around his waist, then he took her into his arms and kissed her.

As if she was a puppet and someone else was pulling the strings, she turned her mouth up to his and closed her eyes.

When his lips brushed hers lightly, longing burst through her with a hungry need for more. While she tightened her arms around his waist, her lips parted. His tongue ran over her lips and common sense vanished.

As she pressed against him, her tongue slid over his and then his mouth came down hard and possessively. She had never been kissed this way in her life, nor had such an explosive reaction to a kiss. She wanted to kiss him the rest of the night. He leaned over her, his strong arms holding her. She felt his erection pressing hard against her as she clung to him.

She didn't know how long she held him and kissed him, until finally, reluctantly, she got her wits together and pushed slightly against him. He straightened to release her. They both gulped for breath as they stared at each other.

"We have to stop," she said. "Neither of us wants

the problems kisses could lead to," she said quietly. "After what I've been through in my broken engagement, I don't want more stress or hurt in my life." Her words were a whisper and she didn't know whether she was telling him or herself.

With an effort she turned and walked away from him, leaving the room to put more distance between them. Her lips still tingled from his kiss. Every inch of her body wanted to be back in his arms, kissing him, being held tightly against his marvelous, strong male body. Desire was intense, but so was caution and memories of how badly she had been hurt not so long ago.

She crossed the hall to look into a mirror. "You are headed for more than a wagonload of trouble. Kiss him again and it'll be a trainload of trouble," she whispered to herself.

She didn't want to be attracted to him for too many reasons. He had no idea who he was. He didn't want to succumb to the attraction any more than she did—maybe a degree more because he was the first to give in to it.

But, oh, what a kiss. Her lips still tingled, her body was hot, she ached for his arms around her and his hard, muscled body against her.

"Sheesh, Ava," she whispered and made a face at herself. "Use your self-control. Do you want another broken heart? No, absolutely not. No, no, no," she told herself. So why couldn't she stop thinking that was the sexiest kiss she had ever experienced?

She threw up her hands. She should go down the

hall to her suite, lock the door and not see him until tomorrow morning, when she would hopefully have forgotten his kiss. Who was she kidding? She'd never forget it, but she needed to resist kissing him again. The minute this storm was over, the water would recede quickly. As soon as she could get back to town, she would take him straight to the sheriff and let the officials take care of him and help him learn his identity. No one lived in a vacuum. And the stranger who had just kissed her senseless was no exception.

What she needed to worry about right now was keeping a distance between herself and him. She didn't want to think about his kisses that had made her heart pound with desire, excitement and a hunger for more. A lot more. She had to avoid him. She didn't want another heartbreak, didn't want to complicate her life. She looked at herself in the mirror. "Can you go back and eat dinner with him and keep away from him?" she asked her image. "I can. I have to," she replied. Taking a deep breath, she turned down the hall.

"I'm back," she said, getting the fish from the oven and getting their drinks and the rest of their dinner on the table.

Sitting across from him, she looked at him. "Kisses won't happen again," she stated firmly, telling herself as much as informing him. "I think you agree— that wasn't the smart thing to do. Neither of us wants another emotional complication in our lives at this time. Right?"

"I'm the one who lost it. I don't want to get into a

relationship when I don't even know who I am." He nodded. "You're right."

"So, then, no more kisses. Let's just eat our dinner and move on," she said, passing him the platter with the fish.

"I apologize for losing control," he said as they shared the tossed salad, baked potatoes and carrots Molly had provided.

Ava looked into his midnight eyes and shook her head. "No, you don't need to apologize. It won't happen again, but believe me, you don't ever have to apologize for that kiss." She felt her cheeks flush and looked down because she was getting back on dangerous ground. She didn't want to think about the sexiest kiss of her life or that he sat only a few feet away.

Maybe it was because of the storm and all the events of the day that it just seemed that way at the time. The instant that thought came she knew better. She was tingly all over just thinking about their kiss. And it didn't have one thing to do with the storm or his rescue or the struggles they'd had getting out of the canyon.

"If you don't want to talk about it, we won't, but was your fiancé someone you had known a long time?"

"We'd been together more than a year," she replied, then paused to take a sip of her water. "We had a big church wedding planned, at least big to me—about two hundred guests. Two weeks before the wedding he told me he had met someone else and it was instant attraction and love."

"Two weeks? Maybe you're better off not married to a guy who would change like that."

She shrugged a shoulder. "Logically, I know that's true. I've told myself that, too, at least a hundred times, but it doesn't make the hurt go away or make any of it easier to accept. I had presents to return, letters to write, people to call. He walked and that was that."

"I see why you don't want any more complications in your life right now." They ate in silence for a bit and then he leaned back. "Well, tell me about how you entertain yourself out here without TV and internet."

Before she could answer, they heard the first ping of hail hitting the house. The hail came faster, the hailstones larger.

"Oh, damn, this must be the next storm coming through," he said. "Thank goodness we didn't have this before you came to my rescue. I'd—"

His words were cut off when a big hailstone smashed through a window on the south side of the room. As glass shattered on the floor, another hailstone broke another window, and she bolted. "I better get towels," she said, rushing from the room.

She could hear another window shatter as baseball-size hailstones struck the glass. She rushed back with towels and went to get a broom and dustpan to sweep up the broken glass.

When she returned, he took the broom from her. "Let me do this."

"I don't think you're supposed to exert yourself."

"I'm not. This is nothing," he said.

She started to argue, but one look at him and she turned away. "I have plywood that will fit the windows and we can fasten it to the window frames with duct tape to keep rain from coming in," she said. "It's on the other side of the porte cochere, in my workshop," she said as she pulled on a thick, tan jacket.

"I'll go with you," he replied, walking with her. She was intensely conscious of him close beside her.

"You may want a jacket because it's cooler out."

He shook his head. "I'm okay."

He was more than okay. He reached out to open the door for her and she smiled at him.

"Thanks," she said, glancing into his brown eyes and feeling as if they had made physical contact. And again, against every one of her warnings to herself, she was instantly conscious of him close by her side, aware it would be just the two of them at her house tonight and maybe several days and nights. The mere thought caused her insides to flutter.

As she passed so close to him, he caught a faint whiff of some enticing perfume. His pulse jumped and he longed to hold her in his arms again. He was very aware of her close by his side as they rushed to the garage without having to get out in the rain and then he followed her into an adjoining workshop.

"There are the sheets of plywood we can put over the windows so it doesn't rain in. I'll get the duct tape and the toolbox," she said and he barely heard her. His gaze went over her face, her smooth soft skin, her rosy mouth. Instantly, he thought about kissing her.

Her kisses were hot, sexy, unforgettable. She bustled around him, getting a big roll of gray duct tape off a shelf, then picking up a toolbox. She put those things down and turned to the stack of thin plywood.

"If you can carry the toolbox and tape," she told him. "I'll take four of these boards just in case another window breaks."

"I'll take the plywood, you get the tools and tape," he said. He picked up the pieces of plywood, watching the sway of her hips as she walked past him. Watching her just made him want her more. He had to leave her alone, avoid hurting her. It was the least he could do, given that she might have saved his life. But it was impossible to stop thinking about holding her and kissing her. He almost groaned aloud.

When they went back to the kitchen, she set down and opened the toolbox. "One winter we had an ice storm and tree limbs snapped and fell. One broke through a window on this end of the cabin and another on the other side. Gerald has a man who works for him who's a good carpenter and they cut this plywood to fit my windows. It should keep out the rain until I can get new windows installed."

"Thank goodness you have it or we'd be floating by morning. Doesn't look like this storm is going to stop any time soon."

"I'm afraid you'll hurt your shoulder if you hold the plywood while I tape it to the window frame," she said as she helped him lean them against a kitchen chair. But he picked up one plywood board and carried it to a window where rain was blowing through the jagged opening.

"I'll be okay," he said as he rested the bottom of the plywood on the window frame. She cut strips of duct tape and stood there seemingly wondering how to get around him to apply the tape.

"Come here, duck under my arm and then you'll be close enough."

He raised his arms and held up the board and she stepped into the circle of his arms to apply the tape. She was as close to him as possible without being against him. As she moved, she brushed against him and he caught another whiff of her perfume. He was too aware that when she had the tape in place on two sides and he could let loose of the plywood, all he had to do to hold her was wrap his arms around her and draw her that last inch or two that separated them. Why was she so tempting to him? His head pounded and his shoulder still ached and he shouldn't feel all this hot attraction that she stirred constantly with no effort on her part. To the contrary, he suspected she didn't want to feel it at all.

She had a huge reason to want to resist any attraction between them. She had been hurt badly. What a jerk she had been engaged to. She deserved better.

He was a total stranger to her and he'd lost his memory. In addition, he looked as if he'd fallen down a mountain, while she was heartbroken over her groom walking out at the final hour before the wedding. They had every reason to feel nothing, even more reason to avoid any kind of attraction. So why couldn't they resist each other?

At this moment, ignoring all common sense, he wanted her in his arms, close against him. He wanted to kiss her again. As he thought about their kisses, he could feel the sweat break out on his forehead.

She glanced at him over her shoulder and ducked under his arm.

"I'll finish taping this one because it isn't tight all the way around," he said, getting another pair of scissors to cut strips of tape. They worked silently and quickly, then moved to the next window and went through the same process again. And again he fought the same urges.

They had one more window after this one. As he stood trying to resist hugging her, he wondered if he would remember for the rest of his life opening his eyes to see a cowboy hat above big blue eyes and golden hair and a beautiful face leaning over him, and his first thought had been to wonder if she was an angel. But, as he'd told her later, angels didn't wear cowboy hats.

His memory was interrupted and he was back in the present as she bumped against him. He held the plywood with one hand while he steadied her with his other hand, placing his hand on her hip. He held her like that for a moment and looked down at her as she looked up at him, and he felt ensnared, unable to move, look away or release her.

His heart drummed and he knew what he should

do. Walk away. He also knew what he wanted to do. Tighten his arm, lean over her and kiss her again.

"I—I need to go," she whispered, breaking the spell she had on him. His hand nearly shook, a faint tremor filled with longing, but he released her.

She was breathing as hard as he was and the look in her eyes indicated she was fighting temptation as much as he was, which just made him want her more.

She shook her head, broke their eye contact as she stepped away.

When she returned, she taped the plywood quickly, working silently.

"There," she announced, then walked away and gathered up the duct tape and the toolbox. "We're finished and now it won't rain in. I'll just get the floor a bit more cleaned up. Thanks for your help."

All the time she had talked, she had looked at the plywood, at the floor, at the other windows on the east side of the room. She hadn't met his gaze at all and he realized she was making a deliberate effort to look away. Which was probably better, considering the sizzling attraction that seemed to flare between them with the least provocation.

He had no idea whether there was a woman in his life, but he was absolutely certain, without remembering anything, that there had never been a sexier kiss than Ava's.

"We'll put this toolbox away tomorrow," she said, setting it on the end of a long kitchen counter. "You sit and watch while I put the dishes in the dishwasher.

It won't take long. Then let's go to the family room and turn on the logs."

"Sounds good to me. But let me help with dishes. I won't do anything that hurts badly or anything strenuous."

Working together, he was conscious of each time he touched her hands with his as he handed dishes to her. He fought the temptation to reach for her and kiss her one more time, certain that there would be another time to follow. It was an effort to keep his hands to himself.

In a short time they went down the hall to a room with tan leather furniture and imitation logs that she turned on in a large stone fireplace with a high mantel. The room was cozy and comfortable with closed shutters, so they couldn't watch the storm, but they could hear the thunder, wind, rain and hail, and he knew the weather would keep him marooned at her place at least through tomorrow.

Above the mantel, he noticed a large framed photograph of horses running in a fenced pasture. "That's a beautiful picture."

"Thank you. That's one way I entertain myself when I'm here. I have a photography hobby."

"You're very good at it," he said, looking again at the picture. "I have no idea if I have any hobbies and I have no idea what interests I have. It's a weird feeling and a very uncomfortable one to not know anything about my life."

"I'm sure. Molly said to let the worries go and relax. Your memory will return."

"That's easier said than done, but I'll try."

"I'm worried about tonight. You have your own suite, but I don't want you to lapse into a coma and no one would know it."

"Oh, Ava, we can solve that one. You're most welcome to join me and keep an eye on me all night long," he drawled and she laughed, a faint sound, and gave him an irresistible smile. A smile that made him want to hold her and kiss her.

"You keep that suggestion to yourself," she replied, laughing again. "We'll not pursue it. What I had in mind is, since I'm the only person with you, I think we should stay awake a bit longer. I don't think you should go off alone yet and I don't think you should go to sleep yet."

He sighed and looked serious again. "Okay, doc. Let's continue to sit in front of the fire. That I can do if it makes you happy."

She smiled at him. "Good. I'm glad you're co-operative."

"For the pretty lady who rescued me, I can be very cooperative," he said to her in a husky voice that changed the moment completely.

"You're flirting again," she whispered as she shook her head. "We weren't going to do that when you don't know what ties you have in your life."

His smile vanished. "You're right. You're constant temptation, Ava," he said softly and lapsed into silence. Why was she such a temptation? From the first moment she had entered his life, and he was aware of her big blue eyes and her silky blond hair, he hadn't been able to keep from wanting to flirt, to touch her, kiss her. She didn't want him to because of the hurt in her past. He knew he shouldn't because he didn't even know his past. So why couldn't he see her as a stranger, a pretty face, a nice person—and nothing more?

He needed to get his attention elsewhere and keep it there. Think about other things and keep busy so he wouldn't be looking at her every second.

He knew that would be easier said than done.

Looking to keep him awake, Ava had an idea. "Want a short tour?"

"Sure," he said, standing when she did.

As they went downstairs to the basement, she talked about when the house was built. She showed him the gym, a big laundry room, the wine cellar, a huge closet with luggage, Christmas decorations and other holiday decorations. Finally, they went back upstairs and every step of the way, she was acutely aware of him. She showed him her library, and the dining room and her office with three computers, two with two screens. She had oak filing cabinets that blended with the oak paneling. Two large desks were at opposite ends of the room. While he looked at the rooms, she looked at him. He was handsome with thickly lashed midnight eyes and thick, black wavy hair. She remembered how he looked when he came back from his shower with his chest bare. And she knew how it felt to be pressed against that muscled chest.

No matter how much she knew she should, she couldn't stop thinking about him and noticing him.

"Looks like you bring your work here with you."

"Not often, but I don't want to have to work and not have what I need here. I did less work when my mother and sister could be here. We all brought friends when I first had this built."

"This is a great place to live, but out here all alone, don't you worry about being here by yourself? This is a big house."

"No. See the light switches by the door? Go flip the switch with the pale blue plate."

When he did, bright lights came on outside, making the yard almost as light as inside the house. Even with the rain, lights were on all over the yard and in trees, illuminating the surroundings.

"Well, I can see why Gerald told you to turn on the outside lights. He can easily see this. I'll turn them off before he gets into his truck and drives over here. But I get it. With these lights you can see what's happening, but you're still isolated."

"I have alarms that will ring at Gerald's. He's not really far away and some of his cowboys are up at all hours. Also, usually when I'm here, he brings over three dogs that I like and they stay with me. They stay in the house at night."

He smiled. "I guess you're not so isolated. Is he bringing the dogs tonight?"

"No, because you're here. You're a good replacement for the dogs," she said and he laughed. He had even white teeth and a dazzling smile.

"I hope that's the first time in my life a woman has told me that." He let out a small laugh and she smiled.

"Now, do you want the upstairs tour or would you prefer to just go back to sit by the fire?"

"Let's sit by the fire."

"Want a cup of hot chocolate?"

"Sure. I'll go to the kitchen with you," he said, walking close beside her to the big white-and-blue kitchen that had state-of-the-art appliances.

"Have a chair and I'll get our cocoa."

"I'll help," he said, following her to a cabinet and watching as she stood on tiptoe to get down white china cups and saucers.

"Let me," he said, reaching up to get the cups, standing close to her and making her think of being in his arms when he had kissed her.

"I know you're doing this because Molly told you to keep me awake. How long did she say to keep me from sleeping?" he asked, leaning against the counter and watching her as she got out the cocoa.

Ava was aware of his proximity and his gaze on her. He was close beside her, his voice a deep, enticing rumble.

"As late as I can," Ava answered, more aware of him standing close than their conversation. "She wasn't emphatic about it because she said this isn't her area of expertise, but she thinks that's what we should do."

"I'll cooperate with you, but I have to tell you, this has been a day with both very good and very bad events. And damn exhausting events."

"I agree. I'm glad I could help, but the storm was terrible and I'm sorry for your injuries and the loss of your belongings. Your memory should return."

"Damn, I hope so. I don't like not knowing who I am or anything else about myself. On the good-news side—I'll heal. Molly said my injuries—the cuts, the blow to my head—shouldn't be too long-lasting or serious. I'll have a scar on my shoulder, though. She said as soon as I can, I should get a CT scan. That's routine, just to make sure my head is okay."

She picked up the cups and turned. At the same time, he turned to face her, and when she looked into his thickly lashed brown eyes, the moment changed. She could remember his kiss and her gaze lowered to his mouth. When she did, her lips parted while her heartbeat sped up. She looked up to meet his gaze again and could see his intent.

She couldn't get out the refusal that she knew she should say. She could barely get her breath. He took the cups from her hands and set them on the counter. His fingers closed on her wrist. The minute he did, she took a deep breath and forgot about the cocoa. She shook her head. "We shouldn't," she whispered, too aware of how close she stood to him. "We agreed we wouldn't."

"One more kiss won't change our lives and it's been a long day. Kissing you was the bright moment," he said in a husky voice. She shook her head, but she leaned slightly toward him and her lips parted again. It had been the best part of the day and she wanted to kiss again, too, even though she knew she shouldn't, that if they kept kissing, it would be tougher to deal with what was ahead. They had no future and she wasn't ready for any relationship. She wasn't ready at all. "I just can't," she whispered, but she stood rooted to the spot, unable to move away, unable to look away.

He leaned closer. "Ava, this has been a hell of a day except for you. If we can catch just a few minutes of bliss, I'm ready to go for it. You're the best thing in my life today. You looked like an angel when I first saw you—I still see you as an angel in my life. Maybe an angel with the hottest kisses. Come here, Ava," he coaxed in a deeper voice, drawing her to him, and she couldn't tell him no when she wanted desperately to kiss him. When his warm lips touched hers, her heart thudded.

His mouth covered hers, claiming her in a fiery kiss, while his arm circled her waist and she kissed him in return.

She finally raised her head. "We shouldn't—"

"Yeah, we should," he whispered, kissing her between words, "and we're not going to cause disasters because of one or two more kisses on a cold, rainy night." He wrapped his arms around her to hold her as he took possession of her mouth again.

She slipped her arms around him, and his hard, muscled body against her felt wonderful. Her heart pounded and she wanted to stop thinking, stop trying to do the smart thing, the right thing, and just kiss for the next hour.

Instead, she thought about how she would get hurt

again. She had no idea what was waiting for him back in his real life.

Seconds, minutes, she didn't know how much time later, but she finally leaned away and he let her go.

Breathing hard, they both gazed at each other for a moment. She turned away from him so she wouldn't go right back into his embrace.

"We have to stop," she said. "I would bet my cabin and land that there is a woman in your life." She took a deep breath and faced him again.

"We can still have cocoa and sit and talk," she said and her words were breathless while her heart still pounded. She wished she sounded light-hearted, just cheerful and friendly, instead of out of breath as badly as if she'd just run a marathon. She couldn't even stop looking at him. She didn't want him to know how she really felt, how attracted she was to him, though she suspected he knew full well.

He took her hand. "C'mon, skip the cocoa. Let's just sit by the fire and talk." He released her hand and she nodded. He left space between them as they went to the family room and sat in front of the gas logs.

She sat in a wooden rocking chair while he sat facing her near the other end of the hearth. Looking solemn, he sat with a lot of space between them.

From outside they heard the distant rumble of thunder and the pitter-patter of rain. It sounded as if the storm was letting up. But she didn't know if this was the third storm predicted, or if another was to come.

He cast his eyes toward the window. "Thank goodness I'm not sitting out on that slope in this weather in the dark with nothing. No shirt, no memory, no wallet or identity—even worse, no marvelous, sexy kisses," he said, and his voice had dropped deeper as he turned to gaze at her with a look that made her hot.

"Are you sure you don't want to come over here and sit by me? That'd keep me awake on this cold, rainy night," he said. This time his voice was lighter and she heard the hint of laughter.

"Thanks, but I'll stay seated right where I am," she answered. "It's safer that way. Especially since, like I said, we don't know if there's a woman sitting somewhere worried about you in this storm."

His smile vanished. "You're right. Well, we will try to do the smart thing so we'll sit by the fire with several feet of space between us." He settled back in his seat. "Go ahead and tell me about yourself. You've told me a little, but I'd like to learn more."

"I'm not that interesting. I've had an ordinary life in a lot of ways. I like helping people, so that's why I have the business that I do. I love kids and want kids in my life. Also, I like my independence, so I enjoy having my own business."

"You sound like a city person, but you have several horse pictures here. How did you get interested in horses?"

"My grandparents had this ranch, so I spent time with them when I was growing up. I've liked horses since I was young."

She talked and he listened, sometimes asking more

questions. After a moment of silence, she focused on him. "When do ranchers put ear tags on calves?"

"When they're born. Why?"

"I just wanted to see how you would answer my question. The answer's not important. What's significant to me is you knew what I was talking about. You didn't have to stop and think about it to answer me. Try this one—what rodeo event do you like best?"

He looked startled and then smiled. "For the first time I remember something. Coming out of the chute during a rodeo. I was riding a horse. I'm glad it wasn't a memory of bull riding." He looked at her intently. "Maybe this is the beginning of the return of my memory."

"We'll hope so."

"Also, it's another small indication that I'm a rancher."

"I agree. If you remember one thing, you might recall something else. Remember, though, Molly said to just relax."

"I can think of some really good ways to relax if you want to help."

She smiled. "You're flirting again. We were going to avoid that."

"You bring it out in me. It's rather harmless so far and a whole lot more fun than trying to jog my memory."

"I think you've stayed awake long enough," she said, standing. "I'll turn off the gas logs, turn out the lights and we'll go to our rooms. If you want me in the night, just call."

One corner of his mouth curled slightly. "You can count on it, darlin'," he drawled. "I can tell you right now if that's all I have to do, you'll get a call."

She smiled. "Stop teasing. You know what I meant. If you have a problem—a real problem that has nothing to do with lust or kisses or crawling into bed together—then don't hesitate to call me. Otherwise, remember all the reasons we should keep our distance from each other."

"Aw, shucks. I thought maybe we would have a fun, memorable night. If it turns out that I'm single, I'm going to want to come back and do this night over."

She smiled again and he came to his feet. She was beginning to think he moved in the same level of society as her family and she wondered where his home was.

When they went to their suites, he walked to the door of his and turned as she started to walk to the door of her suite. His fingers closed lightly on her forearm. "Come here, I want to tell you something," he whispered in a husky, sexy drawl that stirred butterflies in her stomach.

"Whatever you have to tell me, I can hear you from here."

"C'mon, Ava," he coaxed in his drawl that kept the flutters going. "Soon, we'll go our separate ways and this night will just be an old memory," he said as he stepped closer. "It's been a bad time in some ways. Kisses help."

She could resist what he was saying to her, but

she couldn't resist the look in his brown eyes. Or her memories. Taking her hand lightly, he drew her into his embrace and wrapped his arms around her. As he pulled her close, she didn't object. Her gaze was held by his and by the look of desire in his eyes. Earlier, she had tried to avoid another kiss, but now her heart raced, her lips tingled and she wanted to be in his arms. She wanted to kiss him and be kissed, to feel desired again after the devastating breakup that had made her feel so inadequate. His kisses made her forget the hurt and embarrassment, the heartache and pain, the colossal rejection.

Finally, she tilted her face up to his and his mouth pressed against hers. Her heartbeat raced while she held him tightly and kissed him in return. As his tongue stroked hers, she wrapped her arms around his narrow waist. He bent over her, kissing her into oblivion, into blazing desire, while she pressed her hips against him. Never had she known kisses as sexy as his. Or as dangerous.

They were playing with dynamite by kissing and everything could blow up in their faces. Did she want to get hurt even more than before? She knew the answer to that one. No, she did not.

Leaning away slightly, she looked up at him. "This is the biggest folly. Go home, find out who you are and what your commitments are. What your lifestyle is. Then we can think about kisses when you have answers about your life. Right now there are too many questions."

He was silent, as if fighting an inner battle. She

fought her own battle, stating what they should do, but wanting to kiss him. From the start he had been a good guy. He had been kind, helpful, trusting and trustworthy. He had been considerate, grateful for what she had done and was doing for him. Her first feelings and judgments about him had been good.

His hand ran down her back, down over her bottom. His hand was light as it drifted over her, but she tingled with his touch. She wanted the barrier of clothing out of their way. She tried to cling to caution, again reminding herself silently that she didn't even know who he was. She shouldn't be kissing him until she knew whom she was kissing. And even then, she didn't want another broken heart.

She stepped away from him while they both were breathless. He looked as if he could devour her. She felt as if she wanted him to.

"I'll say good night now and I'll see you in the morning. And not before," she said, walking away and too aware he stood watching her. He looked as solemn as she felt. His teasing, flirting and ready smiles had vanished.

"You can come tuck me in and make sure that I'm doing the best for my injuries," he said in a deep voice.

Glad he was back to teasing, she turned to smile at him. "You're doing fine without my help," she said. "I hope you wake up tomorrow and remember your past and your current status. I'm glad I could help you today." She blew him a kiss. "Goodnight, stranger," she said, hoping to remind him of one big reason why the night had to end this way.

She stepped into her suite, closed the door and closed her eyes, momentarily remembering his kisses that had nearly melted all her resistance. He was far too good-looking and sexy. She knew as soon as Gerald got through to the sheriff, they might have answers about her new houseguest. A houseguest who had the sexiest kisses she had ever experienced.

How much longer could she guard her heart and continue to resist him?

# Four

"Bill Smith," he said softly as he looked at himself in the mirror. But that name, or any other, didn't spark any memory.

He walked over to the bed, removed his boots and shed his shirt. Instead of lying back, he sat there, his hands on his thighs, thinking of the woman who'd just walked away. Ava had called him "stranger," to remind him of his status and why they shouldn't kiss. He didn't have any memories, but he couldn't imagine he had known any woman who was sexier than Ava. She set him on fire with her kisses. He wanted her—in his arms and in his bed for the rest of the night. But Ava had been hurt badly by the jerk who walked out on her, and he didn't want to hurt her further. Especially when she might have saved his life.

He could have been in bad shape out in the storm all night in a canyon, where trees were uprooting and falling and land was sliding down into the swelling creek that ran through that canyon. He wouldn't have had anything to eat and no potable water to drink. No way to defend himself against any sizable wild animals. There were probably coyotes, snakes and heaven knew what else out there.

Instead, here he was in this comfortable suite. Until this storm was over and the creeks and rivers went down. Thanks to Ava Carter.

Ava. Her big blue eyes captivated him and her silky blond hair made him ache to touch it. He knew he shouldn't, but he couldn't keep from wanting her naked in his arms.

But every bit of wisdom he could summon told him to avoid intimacy at all costs. He didn't want to hurt her in any way.

She was beautiful, capable, kind, intelligent and oh, so incredibly desirable and sexy. Just the thought of her made him break into a sweat and wipe his forehead. He could get hot, physically hot, hard and ready, just thinking about her.

He hoped that his memory would return soon. It couldn't be too soon to suit him.

Who was he and where did he come from? Who was in his life? The questions plagued him. Molly had told him to let it go. To relax and let nature take its course.

She said not to push it trying to remember. But he couldn't go on like this forever.

He looked at his hands. He had one small scar on

the back of his left hand, and calluses on both. Because of that, they seemed convinced that he was a rancher. Or a cowboy. Plus, he remembered coming out of a chute on a horse at a rodeo. But how could he be certain?

Restless, he stood and paced around the room, then switched off the lights to go stand at the window. Constant lightning lit up the yard. She had lots of trees and landscaping in her fenced-in yard that probably hid rattlesnakes.

That thought surprised him and he didn't know where it came from. He had to be a Texan. Why would he think about rattlesnakes? His head still pounded and he reminded himself again that Molly had told him to try to avoid stress and worrying about his memory loss.

He sighed and wished Ava was here with him. A night together would surely keep him positive and relaxed. Oh, man, a night with Ava. What a thought. Not one conducive to sleep and peace of mind.

He walked back to the bed, propped up pillows and stretched out to watch the rain. He was physically tired, but his mind was whirring and he knew sleep wouldn't come for a while. He wanted to sink into thoughts about Ava and recall each breathtaking kiss that made him want one hundred more, made him want to get to know her. Really get to know her.

He closed his eyes, taking the memory further and envisioning her soft body pressed against him as he carried her to bed and made love to her for hours. Then, they'd sleep, and eventually wake up, and he would take her again.

He raked a hand down his face. Why was he tor-turing himself? He needed to leave her alone. He needed to get his memory back or use what wits he still had and get out of her life as soon as possible.

"Damn," he whispered in the silent darkness and wondered if she was doing as poorly at sleeping. He hoped with all his heart they weren't isolated, shut away in her cabin for days. If they were, could he ex-ercise enough self-control?

If she changed her mind about sex, would it com-plicate his life terribly? There was no way he could say no to her. He tried to shift his thoughts elsewhere because that line of thinking wasn't going to help him drift off to sleep. He got up and walked over to the mirror, looking at himself again, hoping that his eyes or his hair or his mouth would remind him of who he was, where he'd come from. It was pure hell not to know what was going on in his life and why he had been out in the boonies in a big storm.

But when he looked in the mirror, he didn't have a clue about himself. He prayed he would wake up to-morrow and have some answers. Despite everything he'd forgotten about himself, he knew he would never forget kissing Ava.

"Leave her alone, buddy. Don't complicate her life or your own," he whispered, wondering if he was way too late for that bit of advice.

Ava woke to the tempting smell of coffee brew-ing and the sound of raindrops hitting her windows. Startled, she sat up and remembered her houseguest and the past day and night. It was still raining, so they would still be cut off from any communication with the outside world. Would this rain last all day? Two days?

She felt that each day that her houseguest couldn't try to contact someone or at least check with the sheriff of Persimmon, the stranger ran a risk of someone missing him badly.

When she recalled his kisses, her pulse jumped. Briefly, she was lost in memories of his strong arms holding her and his kisses demolishing the defenses she had kept around her heart. She had avoided getting involved with another man since her engagement crash. Until now. She'd taken foolish risks in kissing the stranger because he was exactly that—a stranger. He didn't know himself and she certainly didn't know anything about him. She stepped out of bed to shower and dress, and then she'd go and see if he was better this morning. Had any of his memories returned?

He was sipping the hot coffee he'd brewed and watching it rain when footsteps caught his attention and Ava walked through the door. When she did, his pulse raced.

Looking gorgeous, she was in jeans and a pink short-sleeved sweater that had two open buttons at the throat. Her straight, silky blond hair fell to her shoulders. She had on cowboy boots and she made his heart pound just looking at her.

"Good morning," he said, standing and smiling at her, fighting the urge to cross the room, wrap his arms around her and kiss her. He tried to remember the lectures he had given himself last night about kissing her and doing anything that might cause her more heartache. Intellectually, he knew what he should do. Physically, he yearned for her. "You look fantastic."

"Thank you. Another rainy day, I see. The coffee smells great," she said, entering the kitchen.

"You sit and I'll get your coffee. What do you want in it?"

"Just black, please," she said, sitting across from where he had been sitting.

He placed a cup of coffee in front of her and went around the table to sit facing her.

"You look a bit better than yesterday. Your black eye has improved slightly and that bump you had is gone. How's the memory?" she asked.

"A few random things that are insignificant. Not people, nothing that's really a help. Before you got up, Gerald stopped by. He said he might take me to Persimmon to the sheriff if we can get out of here. Judging from the pouring rain and what you've told me, I don't think we can get out."

"I know you can't and Gerald knows it, too. The rain has to stop and then the water has to run off and the creeks and streams go down. Just relax. We'll try to find something fun to do," she said, smiling at him and he smiled in return.

"May I make a suggestion?"

"I don't think so, unless it doesn't involve both of us and anything where we would touch each other."

"Well, you never want to hear my suggestions.

They were good rainy-day ones," he said. "It would just put a bit of fun into our lives and I don't have to even know who I am to participate and have a great time. You don't have to do anything, but just be your irresistible self."

"I think we should avoid temptation and move on to other topics."

He sighed. "I know you're right and have spent more than half my waking hours since we last talked lecturing myself and promising myself I wouldn't do what I just did—tell you I want to kiss you. So much for common sense. I'll try to do better. We can talk about the rain or you can tell me more of your life history. I can't tell you anything. I'm a blank."

"Not really. You have ideas."

"Oh, yeah, do I ever," he said and smiled. "See what I mean? You bring that out in me." He tried to keep the conversation light, but that wasn't the way he felt. He wanted her in his arms and he wanted to kiss her. Right now, while he looked at her, his heartbeat was faster. They sat looking intently at each other and he realized she was fighting desire just the same as he was.

"What do you do to entertain yourself here?" he asked as he sipped coffee.

"Ride one of my horses sometimes, which is out now. I garden, which is also out. I have a gym and I exercise most days. I run on the treadmill each day. Sometimes I bake things to freeze and take back to Dallas with me. Or I get my camera and take pictures."

"If they're anything like the one over the mantel, they're good."

"Thank you. I have good subjects—my horses, Gerald's, too, a roadrunner who hangs out here in the summer, owls that are here year-round, a pair of cardinals. Once I caught a mountain lion going through." She stood and he came to his feet.

"I'll start getting breakfast," she said.

"I'll help. What can I do?"

"I'll scramble eggs and you pour orange juice," she said. She walked around the table and they both crossed to the kitchen counter and cabinets. He glanced down at her to catch her looking up at him, and when she did, he knew she wasn't thinking about breakfast.

He reached out to take her wrist, but her words stopped him.

"Breakfast, remember?"

"No, I don't remember," he replied in a deeper voice as he tugged lightly on her wrist to get her closer. "I can only think about one thing. Kissing you again." He drew her to him. "Even just a good-morning kiss."

She wound her arms around his waist. "You know we shouldn't. At the same time, you know I can't resist you," she whispered. She turned her face up to his and her big blue eyes were filled with obvious desire, making his heartrate quicken.

He leaned down to kiss her and with the merest contact, all his good intentions from last night were forgotten. He knew he shouldn't be kissing her now, but when he'd finally fallen asleep last night, he'd dreamed about her, and woke up wanting her. He knew she would be out of his life soon and he wanted as much of her as he could have when she was beside him. And kisses weren't binding.

Never breaking contact with her lips, he picked her up. She put her hand on his good shoulder while he carried her to a chair and sat with her on his lap, holding her close against him with one arm, cradling her against his good shoulder. His other hand slipped beneath her pink sweater to push away her lacy bra and fondle her breast, her softness making him ache with wanting her naked in his arms. He caressed her lightly. Every touch, kiss and whisper made him want her more.

She moaned softly as she settled in his embrace. Her kiss was fantastic, blazing hot. Her hands fluttered over him, making him want all of her. His hard erection pressed against her hip as he held her tightly.

When his hand slipped down to unfasten her belt, she caught his wrist and sat up. She was breathing as hard as he was. He felt on fire with longing and need, for all of her, and wanted to carry her off to bed, her naked body against his. But he saw the determined look on her beautiful face.

"We need to have some space here," she whispered and he released her. She stood and walked away.

Pulling her pink sweater back in place, she turned to face him. "I think you know why I want to stop. I'll be back in a minute."

He stretched and took deep breaths as she left the

room. He needed to think about something besides seducing her. Had he ever wanted a woman to the extent he desired Ava?

He looked out the window and tried to think about the storm. Was anyone out there somewhere, looking for him?

It was just lust, Ava told herself as she escaped down the hall. He was an incredibly sexy man—one who clearly wanted to make love to her. Her eager response to him was no doubt due to her being alone so much. And, she acknowledged, perhaps part of it was longing to stop some of the hurt over her broken engagement. It was a way to put an end to being so vulnerable.

She shut the door to her suite, and as she brushed her hair, she lectured herself to get it together and exercise self-control. When she heard a car, she looked outside. Recognizing Gerald's pickup, she went to greet him.

With his hat pushed back to reveal his thick blond curls, Gerald was already inside, talking to her guest, as she entered the kitchen. He looked strong and cheerful.

"We've got spotty showers predicted all day, so the water won't recede, but I thought I'd pick you two up and take you to my place. I'll show Bill some of my horses. You two can spend the day with us today."

When Ava started to protest, Gerald held up his hand. "We insist. Molly has already cooked a bunch of stuff, so get your raincoats, lock up and let's go.

It's just drizzling right now so let's go while the rain is light. I can't go home without you."

She knew he meant it and they were sincere about the invitation. She was relieved because it was a constant, sheer temptation to be here alone with her guest. Going to the Roan house would work better and she wouldn't have to worry as much about what she was doing.

"Thanks, Gerald. I can drive to your place and then you won't have to come out again later."

"Naw, c'mon. I'll be out for one reason or another, anyway, so I'll bring you home. Do what you want here. I'll have a cup of coffee while I wait," he said, getting his coffee. The two men sat talking while she put away a few things. As soon as she finished, she went to get what she wanted to take with her and to put on her raincoat. She found an old slicker for Bill Smith. She still thought of him as a stranger, but she was beginning to feel that he was far from being a stranger to any of them.

"I'm ready," she said when she returned to the kitchen and held out the slicker and an old cowboy hat for her guest. He stood to put them on and the way he slid on the hat, catching his tangle of black hair that fell on his forehead, she had the feeling he had worn broad-brimmed cowboy hats before, and that strip of pale skin on his forehead indicated that, too. In minutes they were in Gerald's pickup on their way to Roan Ranch.

After a big breakfast with the family except the grandmother who had returned to her own house to catch up on her sleep, Bill Smith, Gerald and his seven-year-old son, Aiden, put on rain gear and left to go to look at the horses while Molly cleaned the kitchen and Ava read stories to their five-year-old, Megan.

The men and Aiden were back in time for a lunch of hamburgers, golden corn on the cob and homemade blackberry cobbler with vanilla ice cream.

"Well, Bill doesn't have many more memories, but I'm sure he's a rancher," Gerald informed them over lunch. "He knows horses and is familiar with ropes, tack, tools and barns."

"I have little glimmers of moments on horseback, moments in barns, but I don't recall anything significant or helpful beyond knowing that I'm familiar with those things." He addressed those remarks to Ava, then turned to Gerald. "I think you have some fine horses."

"You're right on that one," Gerald said. "I do. Fine, expensive horses," he added as he smiled.

After lunch the men left again and Molly, Ava and Megan had a quiet afternoon. Ava sat on the floor to play with Megan and her dolls while Molly got dinner ready. When Megan took a nap, Ava and Molly sat talking and later Ava watched Megan draw and color.

The men returned and while the kids went off to play, the adults sat down with glasses of iced tea and some cheese and crackers.

"We drove back to the bridge over Blue Creek," Gerald said. "There's no getting across it today and probably not tomorrow, either. Water is over the bridge, and for about a quarter of a mile approaching it on either side, the road is underwater. Now it looks like a lake down there with roads running into the lake. Doesn't look promising for getting into town. Not until the rain stops and the water goes down."

That night, after a big dinner of baked chicken, mashed potatoes and gravy, home-grown okra and tomatoes, they sat in the family room and talked until about eight o'clock, when Ava said they should go. She felt they had imposed on her neighbors' hospitality long enough.

After goodbyes, Gerald drove them home.

As soon as they watched him drive away and they had stepped inside and locked up, her guest turned to Ava. "Once again, they're very good neighbors."

"They really are. The kids are cute and polite and fun. I love having them for my neighbors."

"I asked Gerald if he ever sold any of his horses and he said yes. I told him if it turns out I'm a rancher, I'm coming back to buy a horse. I may not have memories of living on a ranch, but I know he has some fine horses."

"He does. I think you are definitely a rancher. Everything points to that."

She studied the stranger who was becoming less and less a stranger to her, but she still couldn't think of him as Bill Smith. Somehow, the name didn't fit. She saw he was looking at her and wondered what he was thinking.

"They asked us to stay at their house tonight," she told him. "I didn't agree because Molly has worked all day to have us there, cooking breakfast, lunch and dinner for us, entertaining us. I felt we needed to give her a chance to catch her breath. That's why we're here."

And her first thought since she'd entered the house was they had another night to spend under the same roof.

The second was wondering if he would kiss her again.

Ava watched Gerald's pickup stop by the gate and her houseguest stepped out and talked to Gerald for a minute, then closed the truck's passenger door and headed toward the house. They had gotten through yesterday without a kiss, mainly because Gerald had come by to pick him up and take him back to Roan Ranch. Gerald thought if Bill Smith spent the day following Gerald around as he worked on the ranch, it might jog Bill's memory. Molly had said it wouldn't hurt to try if Bill was willing. He'd been very willing, so he'd left early and then stayed at the Roans' ranch last night because the rain had ended. Today they'd hoped to get across the creek and go to Persimmon to see the sheriff. Today was the first day Gerald could get through to the sheriff and he made an appointment for Bill and let the sheriff know briefly about Bill. Now she was eager to hear if there had been any announcements regarding a missing man.

With a sack in his hand, Bill Smith came up the porch steps two at a time. Her pulse jumped when she saw the unusual expression on his face. "What is it?"

"Come on, we can talk inside," he said, taking her wrist and leading her in.

The minute they stepped into her entryway, he turned to take her into his arms.

"There's only one thing I could think about all the way back here." As his mouth covered hers and he leaned over her, she pressed against him. His body was warm, all hard muscles and flat planes, and he felt perfect. While his strong arms held her, her heart raced. She clung to him tightly and kissed him in return, then stopped worrying about what she should or should not be doing.

At some point, he leaned away slightly and looked down.

"That kiss was the most important thing on my mind." Finally, he released her. "The next most important—I know who I am."

# Five

"Sort of," he added.

She tilted her head to study him and frowned. "What do you mean by 'sort of'?"

"I have a name, but it means no more to me than Bill Smith. There's more news—we still can't get to the Interstate or much beyond Persimmon because part of the bridge was damaged by a tree floating down Blue Creek."

She waved away his latest words. "I don't care about the creek. For heaven's sake, tell me what your name is."

"Okay, I'll give you my name, but it'll mean as much to you as it does to me. I still don't have my memory, but at least the sheriff told me who I am."

She smiled. "So who are you?"

She looked into his dark brown eyes as he watched her. "I'm Wynn Sterling from Dallas, Texas. And it doesn't mean any more to me right now than Bill Smith, except it's my real identity and I do have a history and a family."

"Are you a Sterling of Sterling Energy?" she asked.

He nodded. "They said I am. That doesn't mean anything to me, either. I don't know Sterling Energy. But apparently I have a twin brother. His name is Wade and he was on television. That's how they found out who I am. The sheriff said Wynn Sterling disappeared driving back to Texas from a resort in Nashville. The storms we had here have been all across the Gulf coast and some worse than what we've had. They think Wynn Sterling might have been swept away in the storm. They said the twin brother, Wade Sterling, cut short his fishing trip to the Gulf coast because of the storm and returned home.

"The sheriff will contact the Dallas police. Gerald said we might not hear today because it's hard to get through on cell phones because of the poor reception out here in the boonies. Gerald and I agreed we weren't going to hang out at the police station all day to wait to hear. If I'm going to hang out, I'd rather be with you than the sheriff."

"That's flattering," she said, smiling at him. "Now you know who you are even if it doesn't mean anything yet. You have family, and a big one—a well-known Texas family. I have heard of the Sterlings. Wynn, you're a prominent Dallas citizen."

"So you say." He raked a hand through his thick

black hair. "Damn, you remember and I don't. That's a hell of a thing."

"Patience. Your memory will return."

"Sorry. Don't stop telling me what you recall."

"I think you're single. I don't think you or your twin is married."

"That's good news."

"I've heard of your family, but I've never met any of you until now. Somehow I thought the brother named Wade was the rancher and the other one wasn't, but I really don't know that much about you."

"That's what Gerald said when we heard the news in town. He said he thought the brother he met was Wade. They met at a rodeo and they talked another time at the Fort Worth stockyards. Before Gerald left, he said he remembered that Wade Sterling and three of his cousins, Luke Grayson, Cal Brand and Jake Reed, contributed millions to build a new rodeo arena in the Fort Worth area. It was built to replace an old arena that burned down. I don't even remember having a twin. I have no memory of my sibling contributing to building a rodeo arena, but if I've ridden in a rodeo before and I'm from a well-fixed family, I don't know why I didn't contribute to building the new arena. More puzzles than answers, I guess." He smiled at her. "I'll tell you what I did do. The police helped and gave me the address and phone number of my parents."

"Did you call them?"

"I did and talked to my mother. It was a tough call. She was so happy I was okay that I don't think she worried about anything else and I couldn't tell her I don't remember her."

"You might have to tell her sometime."

"I hope to get my memory back before I see her. Anyway, I have my parents' address. That's where I'll go when I get to Dallas."

"Did you tell them you're coming home?"

"Yes, I did. I told them that because of torrential rains it might be a few days, that I would let them know when I start home."

"I need a car to get home, and I need a license. Not to mention, I don't have a clue where I live. I have my parents' address, but not my own."

"Don't worry, you'll be able to get directions from your family and I'll take you home. We can go together. I'm not doing anything except riding out the storm and the worst of that is over, and the water will go down even more today. We can probably safely leave tomorrow if you don't mind waiting that long. We can try today, but there are still showers and the ground is soaked. I'd rather wait until tomorrow."

"I hate to impose on you to take me home."

"Not a problem. I'm eager for you to get home to your family and find out about yourself."

"Well, thanks. I'll go shower now. If you want to continue this conversation, I'd be more than happy to have you join me."

She laughed as she shook her head. "You don't stop trying, do you?"

He smiled in return. "Not with you, I don't," he said softly and she was conscious only of him and how near he stood. She forgot about his identity and the problems they each had.

His dark brown eyes conveyed blazing desire. It was so obvious it made her weak in the knees. She couldn't look away; she couldn't get her breath. His eyes narrowed just the tiniest fraction, and then he stepped the short distance between them to slide one arm around her waist.

Her heart pounded as she placed her hands lightly against his chest and slid them down around his waist to avoid hurting his shoulder. His dark eyes were filled with desire as his arms tightened around her. His mouth covered hers and their tongues met.

Holding her tightly, he kissed her with a deep insistence. As he did, he tugged her blue denim shirt out of her jeans. His hand went beneath her shirt to push away her bra and fondle her breast. Light touches by his warm, callused hand made her want more.

Clinging to him with her arms around him, she moaned softly as he caressed her. He picked her up to carry her to his bedroom, where he stood her on her feet while he kissed her.

Finally, he yanked the covers off the bed and began to unfasten her jeans. She put her hand over his and looked up at him with hooded eyes that didn't hide the desire consuming her.

"I've been hurt badly and where we're headed, I could get hurt again. I have to wait until you know more about yourself."

"Oh, damn," he said softly and turned away.

She left him, walking to her suite. She knew she

was right and she was trying to guard her heart even if it was too little, too late. She couldn't fathom how important he had become to her.

She had to do a better job of guarding her heart or she would have another painful event to go through when they parted. Or was it already too late?

She groaned and paced the suite, trying to think about something aside from how badly she wanted to go find him and walk right back into his embrace. She wanted to go to bed with him and make love through the night. But that was the sure way to another ghastly letdown. She shook her head. She was already too involved, but she could get over the kisses. If they made love, she would go through heartbreak again because her emotions were invested in physical intimacy.

She had made one colossal mistake but couldn't make another.

If she would just stay out of his bed, out of his embrace and stop kissing him, she might be able to avoid more terrible heartache. That was just good sense, so why was it so hard to do?

She knew the answer to that one. He was incredibly appealing and sexy. She wanted to make love with him. And she knew he desired her. From their first hours, sparks flew every time they were together.

She groaned and changed clothes. Maybe she could slip down to her gym and work out, so she could get some of the longing for him out of her system. If he knew where she was, she hoped he had the good sense to stay away. If they avoided each other more, there wouldn't be that constant temptation to kiss. Right now, she needed to move around and get her mind off him. Wynn Sterling. From a wealthy old Dallas family. Beyond that, she didn't know much about him.

She rushed around the room, changing to shorts and a red T-shirt, then put her hair in a ponytail and peeped out of her suite. She hurried past empty rooms to the basement. She didn't know where he was, but she was glad they hadn't encountered each other.

She rushed into the gym and he was across the room from her running on a treadmill. For just an instant, she started to leave, but she needed a workout. Evidently he had the same idea and probably for the same reason.

She thought about Molly telling him to take it easy. Running on a treadmill was not "taking it easy." Well, she wasn't going to stop him. Right now what she needed more was to cool down her body. She still tingled from their kisses and his hands on her.

That thought did it for her and she rushed to get on a treadmill as far from him as she could get. In minutes she was running. Unfortunately there was no way to get him out of her thoughts.

Wynn Sterling. Tomorrow she would take him home and he would walk out of her life. She had no future with him even if he wanted one because she wasn't ready to risk her heart again. The pain from her breakup had been monumental, coming as it did two weeks before she was to become a bride. She wouldn't trust her heart to anyone again. Not at this point in her life. And if she could keep her wits about her for another twenty-four hours, she wouldn't go to bed with him because it would be much easier to say goodbye tomorrow.

After they parted she didn't expect to see him again. He had another life, a real one, and he was going back to it and out of her life forever, she was certain.

They'd been thrown together by a storm, but she needed to get a grip, resist his appeal and let him go because there could be only one outcome to seduction—heartbreak. *Her* heart. If only she could do the sensible thing—resist him. One more day and then he would be out of her life.

"Wynn Sterling," he said quietly as he ran. The name was meaningless to him. It didn't jog his memory, sound familiar or seem right. He was as blank as ever about his identity, except he had been told that was his name and he was a twin. Sheriff Ellison had recorded the TV clip with his twin and they had replayed it several times for him. They were identical twins. It was like looking in a mirror to look at Wade Sterling.

He had been lost in thought about the name and that it did not trigger even a tiny memory when the door opened and Ava stepped in.

He was surprised that she had also decided to work out because he thought she was going to avoid him.

But he sure appreciated the way she had dressed. She was in a clinging red T-shirt and tan shorts. Short shorts. She had long shapely legs that were to die for.

The sight of her dazzled him. He wanted her and to-night would be their last night together unless more rain came.

When he returned to his real life, he knew he wouldn't see her. She didn't want an affair and he could understand why, at this point in her life. He wondered what his family was like and how he fit into the Sterling clan. Would getting back with them jog his memory? What kind of relationship did he have with his twin? He had no family memories, but he hoped they were close. Were they looking for him now? Were they worrying about him?

Right now he couldn't even speculate about the family that he might find at home. He couldn't keep from feeling he would do better when he was home with his family. It had to help his memory to be in familiar surroundings with people he had known all his life.

Out of the corner of his eye he saw Ava and the vision of her distracted him from his thoughts. She excited him and she had the hottest kisses he could imagine. She had him on fire now and he was going to run until he stopped thinking about kissing her. He had a feeling he was going to have a long run. Was that why she was here?

That thought wasn't conducive to forgetting their kisses, either.

He slowed and finally stopped, getting off the treadmill and moving to a stationary bike.

The bikes were behind her so he could watch her run while he pedaled and that was a delightful sight.

She was a good-looking woman with a sexy ass, spectacular long, shapely legs that he could enjoy looking at for the rest of the day. He wondered if he'd get the chance to touch those gorgeous legs later and feel her smooth, soft skin. He shook his head as he pedaled faster. What was he thinking? He should leave her alone. Twenty-four hours and they would say goodbye.

He swore and tried to think of something else, but he didn't have much in the way of memories. Instead, he was mesmerized by her blond ponytail swaying as she ran.

He groaned. He needed to get back on the treadmill because that view didn't stir sexual images like the one from the bicycle did.

Tomorrow she would drive him home to Dallas. That meant nothing to him. He couldn't envision his childhood home or where he lived now or any of his family. Instead, he had come to feel comfortable here with Ava.

As he ran, he remembered sitting on a porch and looking out over a fenced lawn. Beyond the fence was a drive and across the wide drive was a fenced pasture with horses. Did he own a ranch, too? Wynn realized he remembered something from his past and that pleased him and filled him with hope that his memory was beginning to return.

Before he could tell Ava, she left. Probably to go shower. That was not a thought to dwell on, either. It would mean more hours of running or riding a bike.

Damn, he wanted her, but he didn't want to cause her more pain.

Finally he left to go shower and clean up. Tomorrow he would tell her goodbye. The more he thought about that, the less he wanted to do it.

They both lived in Dallas. Could they continue to see each other? But he had no idea what he was going home to and what commitments he might have. He couldn't keep from feeling that tonight would be his last time with her. Dejected, he left the suite to go find her and see if he could help with dinner.

When he walked into the kitchen, he drew a deep breath. She had changed into a clinging, short-sleeved red sweater that was tucked into the waist of her tight jeans. Her hair, golden and silky-looking, fell freely on either side of her face, and she took his breath away just to look at her. He wanted to walk up, wrap his arms around her and kiss her. He wanted to carry her to bed. His heart pounded. She was watching the door and probably heard his approach.

He crossed the room to her and got a subtle hint of perfume, but he was lost in her big blue eyes. Her soft lips parted slightly as they stared at each other. "You look gorgeous," he said in a rasp. It took all his self-control to avoid touching her. He yearned to pick her up, carry her to his bedroom and peel off those sexy clothes so he could touch, kiss and make love to her all night.

For a moment they looked at each other. She took a step back as she continued to gaze up at him.

They gazed at each other as if caught in a spell that neither one wanted to break.

"You clean up rather well yourself," Ava finally told him, her heart pounding. His black hair was combed and still looked damp, a few unruly locks on his forehead. He wore clothes from Gerald—a blue denim shirt and jeans—and he looked incredibly handsome and sexy. Though she could look at him forever, she needed to move away, to stop staring at him and to stop thinking about tonight—the last night they would be together.

He followed her to the window. A steady light rain fell again. Any precipitation was enough to make a difference in ground already soaked and standing in water. "You may have to postpone leaving here," she whispered and turned to look up at him. He had walked up right behind her, looking over her shoulder. The minute she looked into his eyes, her breath caught. Desire filled his eyes, a hunger for kisses that she felt, too. She couldn't get her breath, couldn't move away or say anything. All she knew was that she wanted to be in his arms and she wanted him to kiss her. He reached out and placed his hand on her waist, then leaned toward her while his gaze lowered to her mouth, and she couldn't get her breath. She couldn't protest or step away or look away. She could only look at his lips and remember his last kiss, which had dazzled her.

"We shouldn't," she whispered.

"I think we should," he answered. "Admit it, Ava, you want to kiss me as much as I do you."

She couldn't deny what he said. His dark gaze devoured her and she trembled, aching to lean a little closer, to feel his arms go around her.

"It's our last night together," she whispered.

"To my way of thinking, it's a last chance for ecstasy," he said in a raspy whisper. His hand slipped around her waist and he drew her to him.

She was going to regret telling him no.

She would regret saying yes.

Which regret did she want to have to live with?

She had to make a choice and take the consequences one way or another.

"What will I have after tonight? I'm not part of your family's world and you still don't know who you really are or your obligations. You know I'll have regrets whichever decision I make," she whispered to him. "If I say yes, I may fall in love and get hurt. If I tell you no, I might regret what I could have had." As she whispered her dilemma, he dropped light kisses on her throat and ear, while he also caressed her breast, slipping his hand beneath her red sweater.

"Then say yes and live with those regrets," he whispered. "And, frankly, I think you've already made your choice. I want you, Ava. I want you with all my being." He showered more light kisses on her and tilted her chin up. She opened her eyes to look into his and her breathing was raspy. There was no mistaking the desire in his expression.

"Yes, I have made a choice," she whispered. "Yes," she repeated as she wrapped her arms around his neck. "Wanting you outweighs the regrets I know

I'll have. This is what I want." She ran her fingers through the hair on the back of his head and pulled him closer to kiss him.

His mouth covered hers and she was lost, spinning away on sensations that made her want all of him, made her want his hands and mouth all over her, made her want to kiss him from head to toe. "I don't know anything about fate and that sort of thing, but being here with you feels like it was meant to be. But, damn, I don't want to do one tiny thing that hurts you. You're a special part of my life, Ava Carter."

"One night isn't going to hurt me. I expect exactly the opposite of hurt tonight."

"Ah, baby, I want to kiss you and touch you for hours," he whispered.

As they kissed, he slipped his hand beneath her red sweater to push away her bra and caress her breast, each sensual touch intensifying her longing for all of him.

He swung her up into his arms and kissed her, walking out of the kitchen and down the hall to her bedroom. Beside her big bed, he stood her on her feet while he kissed her.

She pushed against him slightly, turning to open a drawer. She waved her hand at the packets that held condoms.

"I bought those for my honeymoon when I thought I was getting married. I didn't want to get pregnant on my honeymoon. So here they are."

He smiled and drew her to him to kiss her again.

Her heart thudded when she looked into his dark

eyes, which were filled with purpose. When he picked her up in his arms, she cried out, "Your shoulder!"

"I'm fine," he said. He sat in a big comfy chair, holding her, and he kissed her, his tongue going over hers.

Her insides clenched and her heartbeat sped up while she held him tightly.

"I feel as if I've waited forever for this," he whispered.

"Good," she replied. "So good." And then she couldn't talk because they were kissing—wild, passionate kisses that made her want all of him. Kisses that gave her a feeling of being desired, loved. She wanted to experience his hands and mouth on her and hers all over him. She knew she probably shouldn't let down her guard with him, but for this last night, before she told him goodbye, she was going to make love and make more memories of him. He needed her to get him home, to take care of him tonight. She needed him to help her through a rough time and he was doing so beyond her wildest dreams. She shifted slightly to drag light kisses across his cheek and jaw, over his prickly beard to his ear.

"You're helping me get over some of the devastating hurt of my fiancé walking out on me," she whispered. "I hope I'm helping you get back into your regular life."

"You're giving me the sexiest kisses and most gorgeous body ever. I want to do everything I can to excite you, to take you to paradise. Come here," he said, drawing her closer and tilting her chin up to look into her eyes, and then his gaze dropped to her mouth and she couldn't get her breath.

"You are the sexiest man I've ever known," she whispered, meaning it, but unaware she had spoken loudly enough for him to hear.

He placed her palm on his chest and she could feel his pounding heart. "That's what you do to me," he said. His arms tightened and he leaned closer to kiss her, a slow, sensual, hot kiss, his tongue stroking hers, moving in and out, mimicking the sex act.

She held him tightly, her fingers going into his thick hair at the back of his head while she kissed him and pressed against him. She wanted him with all her being and she had already made her decision. Wise or foolish, she didn't care. She wanted him to make love to her all night long. Why did she feel this closeness with him that she couldn't explain? She barely knew him, yet she felt as if she had known him always.

He was erasing the hurt in her life. She might get hurt by him, but she'd walked into this one, knowing what she was doing and what to expect and not expect from him.

She couldn't be in love with him when she had only known him a few days. This was lust and a hunger for happiness, to forget her broken engagement and shattered promises and hurt. He was strong, upbeat and sexy, and she wanted a night in his arms.

# Six

Closing her eyes as they kissed, she clung to him. He shifted and his hand slipped beneath her sweater to caress her breast, sending tingles that rocked her and made her want more. So much more. And he obliged. He leaned back, his gaze on her, as he watched her while he took the hem of her sweater and drew it over her head.

Longing made her shake, but she, too, wanted the barriers of clothing between them gone. As he caressed her, she unbuttoned his shirt and pushed it off, taking care to lift it off his bandaged shoulder.

"Wynn," she whispered, touching his back. "Your kisses make me forget your shoulder. You may hurt it a lot worse—"

"Forget my shoulder. I'll tell you if we need to

change something or stop. Don't worry about it." He slipped his arm around her waist to kiss her—another long, hot kiss that erased all her worries.

He had tossed away her bra and cupped first one breast in his hand, then the other. His tongue drew wet circles on each sensitive nipple and she gasped with pleasure, while she ran her hands over his hard abs and slid them down to unbuckle his belt and reach for his jeans.

As his hungry gaze went slowly over her bare breasts, he moved her off his lap. He stepped away and when she looked into his dark eyes, her pulse jumped and raced. Desire was blatant in his expression. Standing, he yanked off first one boot and then the other and tossed them aside. He threw his socks on the boots and she moved to unfasten his jeans. She had stepped out of her shoes and there was no mistaking what he wanted. Her heart raced and she tingled, wanting him to take all night, to touch and kiss her into oblivion. She wanted him to make love and kiss her from head to toe, and she suspected that was one wish that would come true tonight.

Her gaze ran over his broad shoulders and desire overwhelmed her. Emboldened, she stood and peeled off lacy panties while he watched her.

The hooded look he gave her, the heat blazing in his eyes, nearly made her gasp. This was desire, the loving and fulfillment she had dreamed of, making her feel cherished, setting her on fire with longing.

When all their clothes were gone, he led her in

front of a Cheval mirror and turned her to look into the mirror.

"You're gorgeous," he whispered. He ran his hand across her breasts and she shifted, turning to look at him over her shoulder. His thick erection was hard, ready for her now, but she wanted to take time. She rubbed her backside against him, closing her eyes and giving herself to sensations that aroused her more.

"Look at us in the mirror," he whispered, his tongue following the curve of her ear while his hands toyed with her nipples and she moaned softly. She was pale against his darker skin and black hair. He was all muscle, fit, ready to make love, his hands running lightly over her and slipping a finger between her legs to find what excited her most.

"You're incredible," he whispered, showering kisses on her nape as he held her close against him.

While his hands caressed her, his hard rod was between her legs, arousing her more, making her want all of him. She reached back to run her hands on his muscled thighs. His strokes rocked her as she moved her hips against him. She gasped with excitement.

"I want to touch you," she said, turning to face him in order to kiss him. She moved away and he let her go, stepping around her to yank back the covers on the bed.

When he turned, his hungry gaze swept over her entire body, then back up to meet her gaze. "You're beautiful. Stunning."

He picked her up again to place her on the bed. The only light was the small table lamp, turned low.

It was a soft, mellow glow that highlighted his muscles and fit male body.

She held her arms out to him. "Come here," she urged in a throaty voice while her heart pounded. He was sexy and incredibly good-looking naked. She wanted to make love all night. She had made her choice and now she wanted to live it, enjoy every second of this last night with him.

He said she'd saved his life. Well, he'd saved her heart and was helping it mend. She would get over her broken engagement now. She would be able to let it go. And that was a gift from him to her. A gift along with the sexiest night possible.

He kneeled beside her on the bed and began to stream kisses on her thighs while one hand played lightly over her, caressing her legs, and the other hand fondled her breasts as he kissed her.

Moaning softly again, she spread her legs for him and he moved between them. He placed her legs over his shoulders, giving him access to her most intimate spot while he showered her with hot, wet kisses along the inside of her thighs, moving higher, kissing her intimately, making her cry out with her arousal.

She closed her eyes while her fingers tangled in his thick hair, her other hand knotting the sheet as desire built.

She grasped his arms and tugged. "I want you now."

"We're just getting started," he whispered. "I want to please you every way possible so you're way more ready than now. I want to kiss and touch every inch of you." And then his hot breath was on her and his tongue was kissing her intimately again, driving her wild with wanting him.

With a cry she wiggled to shift away and he let her go instantly. She sat up and pushed him down on the bed. "I want to kiss you the way you've kissed me," she whispered to him, slipping her leg over him to sit astride him and hold his thick rod, running her fingers across his chest and belly and then leaning down to slide her tongue over him.

He had the fingers of one hand in her hair. His other hand caressed her breast, circling her taut nipple lightly. "You're so soft," he whispered. "Beautiful and soft."

She glanced at him to see his gaze going over her and then looking into her eyes, and she wanted him more than she thought it was possible to desire someone.

She leaned down again to run her tongue over the satiny tip of his erection and then to take him into her mouth. He let her do what she wanted for a few seconds and then he pulled her up, putting her on his lap to sit facing him. She had her legs spread on either side of him and he could fondle her, touch her, shower kisses on her throat while his hands caressed and rubbed her.

"Love me," she whispered. "I'm so ready."

"Soon."

He sat up and put a hand in her hair to tug lightly and then he leaned forward to kiss her, another possessive kiss that made her tremble with wanting him. His arm tightened around her waist, holding her on his lap while he continued to tease her with light intimate strokes between her legs.

She closed her eyes against the overwhelming sensations. "I'm ready and you are, too," she told him as erotic longings streaked from his fingers between her legs. "Make love to me now."

"Just wait a little longer. You like this. You want my hands on you, don't you?"

"Yes, oh, yes," she said, gasping as he continued.

"It excites me to excite you," he said gruffly.

He looked down at her and she met his eyes. The hungry expression she saw there took her breath away. She had never felt so intensely desired.

This was sex beyond her wildest dreams because he was totally focused on giving her pleasure—and did he succeed. He gave himself to sizzling passion that heightened her need for release. She thrust against his warm fingers when he rubbed her soft folds, causing tension that rocked her. Her need for more of him grew stronger, undeniable.

She wanted to give back to him as much loving as she had received. She wanted to make him shake with longing as she did.

He wrapped his arms around her, drawing her to him, leaning over her as she clung to him. He kissed her, a thorough, passionate kiss that made her feel she couldn't possibly be more desired. If she didn't know better, she would have thought it was a scalding kiss of deep, mutual love.

She did know better, though, and realized there was no such thing between them.

And then she stopped thinking and gave herself to kissing him back as passionately as he kissed her. While he continued to kiss her, he picked her up and laid her down on the bed. Then he reached for one of the packets she'd put on the nightstand and opened it. When he returned to her, he kneeled between her legs to put on the condom.

Her gaze ran over him and her heart raced. She wanted him, this virile, handsome and sexy man. Tomorrow he would go out of her life forever, but she didn't want to think about that now.

He lowered himself, holding his weight off of her as he kissed her. Careful of his injured shoulder, she wrapped her arms around him, running her hands over his muscled bare back down over his narrow waist, then down farther over his trim, hard butt.

He paused, looking into her eyes, and then he entered her slowly and she gasped, closing her eyes and holding him tightly.

He pulled away and she moaned, tugging at his good shoulder. "Now…" she whispered. He thrust into her slowly again and she arched her hips to give him access. Sliding one arm under her to hold her, he began to move, slowly at first as she arched beneath him.

His thrusts started to come faster and she kept up with him, moving to his rhythm.

"Put your legs around me," he whispered and she did as he asked.

She was caught in a rising spiral of sensations and

need, tension building as he moved deeper, pumped faster.

Clinging to him, she felt her world narrow to knowledge of only him, his strong body driving her wild, tension still building while she moved with him.

With a burst of ecstasy, she climaxed, crying out in her shattering release as waves of intense pleasure rocked her. He shuddered with his own climax as he continued to thrust, hard and fast.

Then, he slowed and stopped, letting his weight down slightly, and he put his mouth by her ear.

"You're marvelous," he whispered, his breath warm on her ear.

She felt swept away in ecstasy. They were united. He held her with his arms under her. Tightening her arms around him, she hugged him, loving every inch of their naked, warm bodies pressed together. His arm slipped beneath her to hold her while he rolled on his side and took her with him.

She stroked his muscled back, his skin damp with sweat. She lay with her eyes closed and let her breathing and pounding heart return to normal. He showered light kisses on her face and then just held her.

With his strong arms around her and his naked body against hers, she was wrapped in euphoria, filled with happiness.

"I want you here in my arms the rest of the night," he said quietly in his deep voice, sounding totally relaxed.

"I won't argue with that one," she whispered, running her hand over his smooth, muscled back. She didn't want to think about anything except making love with him. It was easier to keep her thoughts only on how sexy he was.

He looked at her and smiled. "I've been thinking," he said. "When I go home, I want you to stay with me at least several nights. If I don't have any commitments, then I'll be free to take you out at night and I would like that very much."

She was surprised because she had decided they would part tomorrow and he would go out of her life forever. She had told herself so many times that he was only in her life temporarily that she'd come to believe it completely.

"Thank you for saying that, but I suspect you're carried away by our lovemaking."

"I meant what I said."

After a few minutes, she sat up and scrambled around to pull the sheet up beneath her arms. "Here's what I'll do. We can drive to Houston and take a plane into Dallas and have a lot shorter traveling time."

"Look, I don't have ten cents—"

"I do and I'll get the plane tickets. You forget that. I have a car at the airport, so I can drive you to your home. I'll call right now and get our reservations."

"That part sounds like a plan," he said. "As long as you stay and have dinner with me. We're going to see each other again," he said in a deep voice.

He ran his index finger along the top of the sheet, his hand moving lightly and slowly over the curves of her breasts, causing tingles up her spine and igniting desire again. She moved his hand away and turned to reach for her cell phone. All the time she made reservations for their flight, he ran his fingers over her lightly. Finally, she finished. "We have a flight, no thanks to you who almost distracted me to the point of giving up my call."

"That call was about tomorrow," he said in the same husky tone he got when he was aroused. "Tomorrow is far away and now I have you in my bed and I want you back in my arms again."

"Gladly. I want you to be happy." They smiled at each other again as she scooted close once more and he wrapped her in his arms.

"You're one big surprise after another in my life," he said.

"I suppose I could say the same about you," she remarked dryly.

He hugged her. "That makes life interesting."

"Mine has certainly gotten interesting since the moment I saw the red taillights ahead through the rain. I tried to catch up with you. I honked, but with the thunder, you probably didn't hear me or paid no attention. You didn't stop or slow down. I know the road and I knew in storms like we had, water would be pouring over the highway and it would be impassable. I was going to turn around and go back, but that's when I saw your taillights. I thought if I could catch you and get your attention before you reached that curve, you would be able to turn around and follow me back."

"I'm glad you didn't catch me. I wouldn't be here with you like this."

"Maybe. You might have been and then you wouldn't have amnesia."

"True." He looked like he was giving that some thought. Then he spoke again. "I think we've talked long enough. Let's go shower."

"I don't know if I have the energy to stand."

"Well, there's a remedy for that," he said, stepping out of bed and turning to pick her up.

"Stop. Put me down before you tear your stitches loose and start bleeding. Don't you hurt?"

"Not holding you, I don't. I'm enjoying your warm, deliciously naked body too much to notice the aches. With you in my arms I don't care if I hurt and I'll bet Molly has me sewn up tight and those stitches will hold. You're a featherweight and it doesn't add to my aches to carry you."

She laughed as she wrapped her arms around his neck. "Okay, if that's what you want and it won't hurt you. I admit I like this better."

"I definitely like it better, too," he said in a deep, husky voice.

As they showered, his hands were all over her, just as hers were all over him. They finally rubbed each other dry with fluffy blue towels and then he drew her into his embrace to kiss her again.

Each kiss seemed to have more impact than the kiss before had. She instantly wanted him again and she knew he wanted her.

He picked her up to carry her back to the bedroom.

"I can walk, you know."

"I can't stand you being that far away from me."

He took her to the bedroom, placed her on the bed and turned to get a condom. As he did, her gaze ran down the length of him and her pulse drummed faster. Naked, he set her body afire. She was ready to make love again and again.

When the first rays of sunrise spilled into the room, she stirred. She turned to look at the man sleeping beside her. How many times had they made love last night? The bigger question was how much of her heart had she given him?

Until they made love, she could have walked away after telling him goodbye and her heart would still have been intact and unbroken.

Now she wondered how deep her feelings ran for him. One night shouldn't be everlasting love. But temporarily, he was part of her life and he was incredibly sexy.

She knew the risks when she'd agreed to go to bed with him. What was done was done and there was no way she could regret the lovemaking they'd shared. He was going to be impossible to forget. She hoped he had a nice family and she hoped his memory returned swiftly. And she hoped with all her heart she hadn't fallen in love with him.

She slipped out of bed and went to shower. When she returned, the bed was empty and she suspected he was in another shower. She left for her own suite to get dressed, but she couldn't keep him from invading her every thought. He was going home to a big family and to discovering all about himself. Did he look forward to it...or did he dread it?

After she dressed, she entered the family room, immediately spotting him standing by the window. Wearing jeans and Gerald's blue-and-red plaid shirt, Wynn turned and his gaze swept over her and he crossed the room to her. Her heartbeat accelerated while she stood watching him, looking into his eyes and knowing he was going to kiss her. While her pulse raced, she felt a flash of desire.

"Remember, we have a plane to catch today. A commercial flight, so we'll have to be on time," she said.

"I'll remember, and this will just be a quick kiss. You look terrific, by the way," he said, taking in her jeans and blue sweater.

"Thank you. You look rather good yourself."

"When I get home, I'm going to give these clothes to charity, but I'll guarantee you, I'm glad to have them now because my own were in tatters." He stepped closer and slipped his arm around her waist.

"Last night was fantastic. The best," he said solemnly.

"I agree." She gazed up at him. "Are you going to kiss me or just keep talking?"

She saw his answer in his expression, and his arms tightened, drawing her into an embrace.

The minute his lips met hers, she wanted nothing more than to hold him, to have him stay with her. To strip off their clothing and cancel their flight. But she knew she had to let him go. He had to get back to his real life.

Finally, she stepped away, smoothing her sweater and trying to catch her breath and cool down. "We're running out of time."

For just a moment she thought he was going to reach for her again, but he let out a long breath and turned away. "Yeah. We need to get to the airport. I need to go find my life and my past."

As she watched him walk away, she thought, *Yes, and I'm not part of either one except for the hours you spent in my cabin.*

Ava drove them to Houston to the nearest airport, parked and they flew the rest of the way into Dallas. They took a shuttle to get her car and then he gave her the addresses he had been given by the sheriff to his Dallas condo as well as his parents' home.

The whole time she tried to avoid thinking about telling him goodbye. They got her car, she put the address of his condo in her GPS and drove to a high-rise building overlooking downtown Dallas. As arranged earlier by the sheriff, Wynn got a key from security and they rode to the penthouse condo.

He was told he had a private entrance and they used it to take the elevator to the fifteenth floor where they stepped out into a hallway. He unlocked his condo door and entered. Sunlight spilled through a wall of windows as they walked through an entryway into a large living area. Walls, furniture and throw rugs were all white, with glass and stainless-steel contemporary furniture.

Wynn paused as he looked around and shook his head. "I don't remember one thing here. I'm not even sure I like it."

"Maybe you'll feel differently after you've been here a while."

He looked around and turned to her to place his hands on her shoulders. "The only thing that looks familiar in here is you. Come here. It's been a long time since we left your place and all I could think about most of the time was getting somewhere alone with you so I can kiss you."

He reached for her and she placed her hand on his chest to push lightly. "Whoa. One kiss only, because you don't have a lot of time. We need to allow thirty minutes to get to your parents' house. You told them you'd be there at five."

"We're wasting some valuable minutes here," he whispered, sliding his arm around her waist to draw her to him and kiss her. With every kiss now, she thought it was a goodbye, but then he found a time and place where they could kiss again. The real good-bye was coming tonight or tomorrow, she was certain. She stopped thinking about it because while his mouth was on hers she couldn't think about anything except his kiss.

While her heart raced, she pushed slightly and looked up at him. "You'll be late getting to your parents' for their family dinner for you tonight. You said you wanted to shower."

"Yeah. Want to join me?"

"You'd never get there for dinner," she answered, shaking her head.

"Okay. I'll go and I'll hurry. I don't even know where the shower is."

"You're a big boy. You'll find it," she said, turning to walk to the glass doors that opened onto a balcony.

She heard his boots as he crossed the room and then she was alone. She walked across the spacious room, saw an open door and walked into a large bedroom with black-and-white decor and an oversize bed with a mirror above the bed. She walked over to a glass table with steel legs. A picture in a silver frame was on the table and she picked it up to look at Wynn and a gorgeous blonde smiling into the camera. His arm was around the woman and she had her hand on his knee and was leaning against him. Her black dress was elegant and looked expensive.

Ava put the picture back. Looking at the picture, she hurt inside, even though common sense made her question if there was a woman in his life.

She glanced around and walked out onto the balcony to look at Dallas spread below, but her thoughts were on Wynn and how tonight might be goodbye.

"I'm ready to go to my folks' house," he said, stepping out on the balcony minutes later, and her heart thudded. His black eye was gone and his bruises had almost faded away. His thick black hair was neatly combed. He wore a crisp white dress shirt, open at the throat, gold cuff links in French cuffs, navy slacks and his same boots, and if she had thought he was handsome before, it was nothing to the way he looked now. Her heart raced and she wanted to touch and kiss him and just look at him.

"Wow, do you clean up good."

"Dang. Now I really do want to call them and tell them I can't get there until tomorrow night."

Laughing, she took his arm. "No, you don't. No telling what they've been doing to get ready for your homecoming. Come on, handsome man, let's go. The sooner you go, maybe the sooner you'll get home."

"Yeah, right. I'm sure not the rancher brother— there isn't a pair of boots in that whole big closet that is filled with clothes. I don't know where or how I got these. I have to tell you, my taste in clothing must have changed with this bump on my head because there are some flashy clothes in that closet that I can't imagine wearing."

She laughed. "On you, I'm sure anything would look good, you handsome devil," she teased.

"I really would like to cancel tonight and go see your house and bedroom and shower."

"Maybe we can work that in later or tomorrow," she said lightly, but she hurt because she thought of the beautiful woman in the picture with him. She could easily be at his parents' home, waiting for his arrival.

As they rode down in the elevator, Ava couldn't keep from looking at him. He still had the shadow of short whiskers on his jaws and chin and the look in his dark eyes made her pulse continue to race.

"I can take my car and use the GPS."

"When you can't remember you parents, I don't think I should let you go on your own. I'll take you this time and I'll be happy to pick you up and take you back to my place or yours," she said, turning to smile at him.

"Oh, baby, I want to turn around now."

"No, your family is waiting. Let's go."

She drove to an older part of Dallas, where homes were mansions, set back from the street with land-scaped yards, tall shade trees and well-tended beds of blooming flowers in the warm Texas fall.

"I'd like you to meet my family. Have dinner with me and my family tonight."

She wanted to say yes, but she didn't think she should. "Thank you. That's nice, but you're going home to your family and you don't know what you'll find. Your memory hasn't returned. You reacquaint yourself with your family. You may have a girlfriend here tonight waiting to see you and that could be awkward if I'm with you."

He rubbed the back of his neck and nodded. "I guess you're right. I'll be with you later tonight. By then I'll know my family and any friends they have join us tonight."

"Maybe seeing where you grew up and your family will begin to trigger memories."

"If it doesn't, I'll be sharing my time between a doctor's office and a home with a bunch of strangers who are my family. I don't even know what kind of work I do."

"I suspect you don't have to worry about it too much."

His family home had a circular drive and she took him to the porch steps of a sprawling three-story mansion with a wide front porch that had white Doric columns.

"Well, here's your parents' house," she said. "Your childhood home, from what we could learn."

While he unbuckled his seatbelt, he looked intently at her and her heart beat faster. Slipping his hand behind her neck, he drew her closer while he leaned toward her and his gaze went to her mouth.

The minute his mouth covered hers, her heart thudded. She closed her eyes and kissed him in return, slipping her hand to the back of his neck. It was a long, breathtaking kiss that made her heart pound and made this parting hurt more.

When he sat back, he looked at her solemnly and she wondered what he was thinking.

"Go get reacquainted with your family."

He glanced over his shoulder at his childhood home. "I'd feel a whole lot better about getting out of this car if you would agree to go out with me tomorrow."

She had to smile at that. "Why don't we discuss that when I pick you up tonight?"

"Tomorrow I'll have money, sweetie, and I can take you out to eat at the fanciest place we can find."

Laughing, she shook her head. "Just go find out about yourself."

"Okay," he said, smiling at her. She reminded herself he had no idea who was waiting in that big house for him. He'd had no past, no ties, and that was about to change completely and she could get a call from him later today canceling tomorrow's plans and telling her goodbye. She wasn't going to think about that until it happened.

"I can't wait for later," he said, giving her a look that made her tingle.

"Call me. You have my number."

He nodded. "Well, I hope I recognize my family and I hope this jogs my memory." He stepped out of her car, closed the door and went up the steps to ring the bell.

She drove away slowly, but looked in her rearview mirror as she went down the circle drive. He was standing at the door and she saw it open and a man greeted him as he stepped inside.

Hurting, she wondered if she had just kissed him goodbye.

# Seven

Wynn stood on the porch and punched a button, hearing chimes play inside, and then a butler opened the door. "Ah, Mr. Wynn, welcome home. We were so happy to hear you're safe."

"Safe, but without any memory, so tell me your name. I don't even remember the house," he said, looking around. But as he studied the surroundings, he had a flash of memory. Walking into this entryway and hall and bringing a woman to dinner with him.

"Oh, my, they told me about your memory loss. I'm George Bolton, the butler. Let me show you to the great room and I'll tell your mother you're here. She and your younger brother, Jack, are home right now. Your sister, Lucy, isn't home yet, nor your dad. He gets in later tonight."

"His sister is home now, George," a cheerful voice said, and he looked down the hall to see a willowy, black-haired woman striding toward him.

"Lucy," he said, a memory coming of catching her when she fell off a horse when they were kids. And then another memory of her running to him when he set a high-school record as quarterback of the football team. And even though George told him, he remembered her name. "Lucy," he said again with more enthusiasm. She was the first person since the blow to his head that he recognized, and he was thrilled.

Relief filled him, along with a warm feeling for his younger sister. He was certain he had always been close to her. He started to hug her, but when he reached out, she shook his hand.

"Welcome home, Wynn," she said solemnly and he stopped, feeling surprised. She didn't really sound happy to see him. He shook her hand carefully and she turned away. "I'm going to my room. I'll see you downstairs at dinner."

"I'll tell your mother that you're here," George repeated and left, walking out behind Lucy.

Wynn looked at his sister walking up the stairs. What kind of dynamic did they have? Her cool greeting indicated she didn't like him, yet his memories of her were so positive. His reactions when he first saw her were warm and friendly. He wished he could tell all this to Ava. Ava was a good listener, with good ideas and clear thinking. Thinking about her, he felt a pang. He already missed her and that startled him. In spite of their intimacy, he barely knew her. And yet, because of their intimacy, she was on his mind a lot.

Now he was beginning to remember his life. Seeing his family and childhood home must have triggered the memories that were coming back to him full force. Relief that he remembered his life was overwhelming and he felt a rush of joy.

After Ava had pulled him out of that canyon in the storm, he hadn't had a clue about anything in his life or who he was. Ava had been the solid rock that had stabilized him, helped him, gotten a nurse for him and given him reassurance and hope. And then given him the sexiest night of his life. He wanted to be with her right now. That surprised him because he had just left her.

Thinking about her made him want her that much more. He wanted Ava in his arms, in his bed tonight. Making love to her was a recent memory and he had full recollection of every moment of that night. Total recall of how soft she was. How sexy she was. How fantastic she was in bed. No faded memories there. He was certain there had been women in his past, but he couldn't imagine any as sexy as Ava. Or as good a friend, even though they had known each other only a few days.

Was he in love?

That thought jolted him. He hadn't known her long enough to be in love. Suddenly another memory came. He didn't want to marry and he didn't want kids. He was as certain of that as he was that Ava had saved his life. And his reason for not wanting kids?

He didn't want them because they might be like his brother. They might be like Wynn. They might be like his brother Wynn.

He ran his hand over the back of his neck as that thought struck him. *His brother Wynn.* "Damn," he said aloud, still standing in the hall by himself. His *brother* was Wynn. *He* was Wade. He closed his eyes as memories filled his mind.

"I have a ranch," he whispered. "I'm a rancher, just like Gerald said." And then he remembered his brother was a troublemaker in a lot of ways. And Wynn wasn't a rancher. He hated ranching.

"Damn." He was Wade Sterling, and he wasn't surprised because he realized now that his brother had been impersonating him. And he remembered it wasn't the first time.

Memories tumbled through his brain. Wynn had done that over and over through the years. Wade felt certain of little snippets of memories, of fighting with Wynn because he had gone out with Wade's girlfriend in high school and told her he was Wade.

And now he remembered that he never wanted to marry and never wanted kids because they might be like his brother. Their dad had had his first stroke when he was fifty-two. Wade thought that was young and he blamed Wynn for causing their dad so many worries. He could remember all of that now. His whole life was coming back to him, pouring back in a rush.

Relief, joy and a huge longing to tell Ava filled him. He wanted to call Ava, so he just gave in to it.

She picked up on the second ring. "Wynn?"

"Ava, I need to talk to you." Without waiting for her response, he launched into the reason for his call. "My memory is coming back."

"Oh, that's wonderful!" He could hear the smile in her voice. "Molly said it would."

"Maybe the house triggered it. I don't know. But, Ava, I have a lot to tell you."

"I can't wait," she said breathlessly and he wondered if she was thinking about their kisses and making love. He hoped so, because he was.

"I'm not staying here tonight. I'll get a car and get back to your house."

"Just call me and I'll come pick you up."

"We'll see. Ava, I'm not Wynn."

"What do you mean? What are you saying?"

"I'm Wade Sterling."

"Wade? The other twin?" She sounded incredulous. "But didn't you say that your twin was on television and he said he was Wade Sterling?"

"That's right. My brother has a warped sense of humor and we don't get along very well."

"Mercy," she said on a gasp. "You do have a lot to tell me later."

"Okay. Talk to you then." Before she could disconnect the call, he quickly added, "Hey, Ava, I miss you."

"I miss you," she said softly. "Really miss you," she repeated with a breathlessness that made him ache to hold her.

"I'll see you later," he said, then ended the call and

put his phone in his pocket. He took a deep breath and stretched, relishing his memories of holding and kissing her last night.

He stood looking at the house, recalling more moments. He was Wade and his brother was Wynn. And his brother had periodically taken his place, not just in high school, but all through their lives. And he'd done it successfully. Wynn had been in all the school plays and was a good actor. As the years went by, he got better at acting and passed himself off as Wade.

"I'm Wade Sterling," he repeated. He thought back to the storm, to going off the highway in a flash flood, his pickup tumbling into the canyon. And he remembered…

"Olivia." He whispered the name. He'd been about to break up with her when all this happened to him. They moved in the same circles, but he had lost interest in her and he felt it was mutual. She seemed as ready to part as he was.

More recollections came back to him. He remembered he liked his younger sister, Lucy, and she had always liked him. The same with his younger brother, Jack. Along with Wade, Lucy and Jack had fought with Wynn all their lives. Now he knew why Lucy had been so cool toward him—she had thought he was Wynn.

And then he remembered he and his cousins, Luke, Cal and Jake had contributed money to build a new arena in Fort Worth. The arena construction was complete, but they needed to plan a grand opening. He needed to call his cousins.

Suddenly his mom came rushing in and hugged him. "Wynn, I'm so glad to see you. My darling Wynn, I've been so worried about you. Dad and I have worried and hoped you'd get home okay. I thought you were going to see your friends in Nashville, so I thought you were safe and Wade was home with us." She hugged him. "My precious baby."

Wade had to laugh as he looked down at her. Her hair was a mass of black curls and her brown eyes weren't dark like his. He recognized the familiar perfume she always wore, year in and year out. "Mom, slow down. I'm fine. I'm home and I'm Wade."

"Oh, darling, you can't remember who you are. George told me you said you lost your memory. You're Wynn. Wade has been home in Dallas with us."

"Mom, I know you can tell us apart if you really look at us. Look at me."

She leaned away and stepped back. She put her hand against her cheek. "Oh, my heavens, you're Wade." He smiled.

"Oh, that naughty boy. Your brother just can't stop his pranks," she said, laughing. "None of us even noticed. We all thought he was you. He copies you well. Well, you're home and fine, so don't be mad at him and his games. I'm sorry you got caught in that terrible storm. Would you like a drink before dinner? The others will be here shortly. George told me Lucy just got here." She frowned. "Oh, dear, if you're Wade, and you are, Olivia is coming with Wynn." She patted his arm. "Now don't get angry with your twin. He likes his little jokes and no one was hurt. You didn't even know that he's been telling us he's you until you arrived here, did you?"

"No, Mom, I didn't know about Wynn's little joke." He didn't hide his sarcastic tone.

"Be nice, Wade. We'll have a party tonight."

"Mom, the woman who saved me and got me out of that canyon in a terrible storm lives here in Dallas. Actually not too far away. She saved my life. I'd like to invite her to dinner tonight and let the family meet her."

"That would be lovely. You should have just brought her with you."

"So you don't mind if I invite her now?"

"We'd be delighted to meet her. By all means, go call her."

"Thanks," he said.

"What about Olivia? Wynn is bringing her tonight."

"And he'll take her home tonight and that's fine."

"Oh, my. He'll have to tell her he's not you."

"Olivia will adjust," he said, certain Olivia already knew.

"Go make your call. If you want a drink, get one. I'm going to see about dinner. Oh, it's so good to have you home. To have all of you here." She laughed and shook her head. "Naughty Wynn. He just can't resist a little fun."

Wade watched her go, hurrying to oversee the Sterlings' first-class cook. His mother loved to cook and putter around in the kitchen and they had lost more than one good cook because of that. That was understandable, since cooking was her hobby. But he couldn't understand why she always forgave and excused Wynn. And if he quizzed her about it, she always said he was just like his uncle, Ethan Sterling, their dad's younger brother. Wade remembered when he'd once asked his dad about their uncle and he said she was correct. Wynn was just like his Uncle Ethan and their mother had dated Ethan first. She had been in love with Ethan when he was killed in a motorcycle wreck.

Wade pulled out his phone and called Ava. His pulse jumped at the sound of her voice.

"Hi. We just talked, so what's up?"

"Mom wants me to invite you to come for dinner. I can't wait to see you. I feel like I told you goodbye hours and hours ago."

She laughed. "Are you sober?"

"Yes, I'm just wound up at the thought of getting you here."

"It'll take me a little while to change."

"That's okay. Text me when you're almost here and I'll go out on the porch and watch for you."

"That's a deal. See you in about an hour, okay?"

"Fine. An hour. And then when you leave, I'll go with you if that's okay with you."

"Of course it's okay," she said in a sultry voice that made him want to be with her right then. "I can't wait."

"Don't tempt me to skip out early. Mom loves having company for dinner."

"Goodbye. I'm going to get ready now."

"I am so ready," he said in a husky voice.

"Oh, my."

Wade smiled. He would be with her soon and with her tonight. All night. Images of their lovemaking last night flashed in his mind, but he banked them before he got aroused.

He tried to calm down and focus on the family and ignore his racing pulse and his eagerness to see her again. How important was she to him? That question startled him. But he had to admit she had become very important. He went upstairs.

He knew where he was and he wanted to go see Lucy if she was in her suite. Relief overwhelmed him that he knew his identity. He would get his life back and a lot more now because Ava was in his life. He looked down at the clothes he was wearing. Not his clothes. He wanted to get his own clothes and his boots.

He passed an open door and when he glanced inside, he knew it was Lucy's suite even though she wasn't in the sitting room. He crossed the room to straighten a picture that periodically slipped and became crooked and it was too high for Lucy to reach unless she stood on a chair, so often he fixed it for her.

He heard her behind him. "I'm fixing your picture. I wanted to talk to you—"

She stared at him and looked at the picture. "You're not Wynn. Oh, my gosh, you're Wade." She dashed across the room to hug him.

He blinked in surprise, then put his arms around

her. "You didn't think so when I first saw you in the hall."

"No," she said, stepping back to smile at him. "I was distracted, but I can tell which one of you I'm with if I really look at you. And you straightened the picture, like you always do. Wynn never once has. Which is all right with me. On Dad's orders, Wynn is supposed to leave my things alone."

He wanted to reach out and hug her again, but she continued. "The whole family thinks you're Wynn. The whole family except Wynn, that is."

"Where is Wynn?"

"He'll be here and he's bringing Olivia." Her hand flew to her face. "Wade, Olivia thinks she's with you. You're the one she's been seeing for the past year. Do you think that's why he did this? He wanted Olivia?"

Wade smiled and squeezed her shoulder. "It'll be all right. Olivia and I were about to split, anyway. I'm glad she's with him."

"You really mean that, don't you?"

"Yes, I do."

Her lips firmed and she wrinkled her brow. "I know you won't lose your temper when we're all together. I worry about Dad getting upset. His doctors told him to avoid stress."

"Well, hell, that went out the window when Wynn was born. I'll talk to Dad and emphasize all the good things—I got home safely, I have my memory. At this point I think that's about all we can do." He shook his head. "I don't know why Wynn has to pull these childish pranks. He needs to grow up." He stopped. "Enough about him.

"On another subject, Mom told me to invite my new friend, Ava Carter. She saved my life in a terrible storm. She saw my pickup sweep off the road and saw me jump before it went down into a canyon. She climbed down to get me out of there, helped me back to the road and took me home with her. We had a hell of a storm that night and I really think she saved my life. I'd lost my memory—probably when I fell—and I didn't know where the pickup was, nor my phone, and I lost my wallet so I had no identification. To top it off, I was cut badly and bleeding."

"Oh, Wade, that's awful."

"I really owe her and I want all of you to meet her. She has no family. Her mother and sister died and she doesn't have contact with her dad."

"I'm glad she took you in, but with no memory— that's a little scary to take a stranger home when you live alone."

He told her about Ava's wonderful neighbors, including Molly, who had tended to his shoulder.

"How is your shoulder?"

"It's mending. I think it's fine. I'll go see our doc and let him check me over because of the head injury and memory loss."

"I'm glad we'll get to meet your friend."

"I'm glad you will, too. Ava is an occupational therapist. Well, sis, I'd like to say hello to Jack. I remember the house and where Jack's suite is located. I'll see you again shortly, probably in the great room."

"Sure. I'm glad you're home, Wade. Real glad."

"Thanks, Lucy," he said. "It's good to be home and beyond good to get my memory back."

She laughed. "Wynn had to behave himself to pose as you. What a relief it was."

"Well, he can be his usual ornery self again."

"I can't wait to meet Ava. If you like her, then I know I'll like her."

"You'll like her, I promise," Wade said, pausing at the open door. He smiled at Lucy and left to go see his baby brother and let him know about Wynn, the imposter.

He more than had a feeling Lucy's theory was right. In fact, he was certain Wynn did it to get Olivia. How long was she fooled? he wondered and smiled because he doubted if it was long at all.

At Jack's suite Wade knocked on the open door and walked in when Jack told him to enter. "Well, you made it back," Jack said with a glance as he pulled neatly folded black and brown socks out of a drawer.

"Looks as if you came home to get a few things."

"That and Mom twisted my arm to get us to come home to welcome you on your first night back."

"Being here in this house, seeing family members— I don't know if that's what did it or if it was just a matter of time, but I have my memory back. I'm not Wynn."

Jack stopped what he was doing and whirled around to stare at him. "You're Wade?" his brother asked, doubt in his voice.

"I think I am."

"Dang. You are," he said, staring at Wade. "You

sure are. I just glanced at you before, but I can always see it if I pay attention and really look. And that's the way you would answer," Jack said. "Wynn would have said, 'I know I am.' That damn Wynn, what did he have to gain other than to fool every—? Oh, wow," he said, suddenly quiet as he stared at Wade. "He wanted Olivia."

"I have no claims on Olivia. I do remember her now, but I'm not interested in settling down with Olivia. Frankly, that's how I realized my identity. The thought came to me that I haven't ever wanted to marry and Olivia was beginning to talk about marriage. I don't want to take the chance on having a kid like Wynn," he said, remembering being with Ava and thinking it would be good to have a baby with her. He looked at his brother. "Jack, that's exactly what ran through my mind and I realized I'm Wade."

Jack shook his head. "I should have caught on. At the time Mom just told me Wade was home and Wynn was in Nashville and I had no reason to doubt that."

"I understand, Jack. Don't blame yourself."

"But, Wade, about that no-kids thing—I've thought that myself sometimes. I don't want to marry someday and have a kid like Wynn. But I realize that isn't going to happen. Neither one of us would have a kid like Wynn, because we wouldn't tolerate his antics, unlike Mom, who thought he was cute and encouraged him."

"That's true," Wade said.

"While you were away he brought Olivia to dinner several times. I gotta say he knows how to impersonate you and it's actually too bad he's going to stop now because he's a whole lot nicer to have around when he's trying to pass himself off as you."

Wade actually laughed at that, as did Jack. He knew it was the truth.

His brother sobered quickly, though. "What about Dad? When this comes out, it may give him another stroke."

"Maybe I can get in touch with Dad and break the news that I'm Wade a little more gently to him."

"I think that would be good. You're perfect for that. Ah, now Wynn will just go back to being his usual rotten self." He shook his head. "I'm amazed Mom didn't fall all over you and cry with joy since she thought you're her darling Wynn."

"I'd already realized I'm Wade. When I told her he's been impersonating me, she just laughed."

"Speaking of Wynn, here he comes."

Wade saw Jack looking out the front window and walked over to watch. He saw his twin get out and circle the car to hold open the door and Olivia stepped out. Wade remembered her and was thankful again that he'd regained his full memory.

He also noticed that Olivia was stunning with her long straight blond hair framing her face. She wore a pale blue dress that clung to a curvy figure and had a short skirt that showed off her legs. The deep vee neckline revealed an ample bosom and a diamond pendant sparkled at her throat.

When he saw her, he could appreciate her beauty, but other than that, he didn't feel anything. Seeing her just made him think about Ava and wish they were through with dinner and he could leave with her.

"I don't know how you can keep from going downstairs and punching him out for telling everyone that he was Wade Sterling. Do you think Olivia will be angry?" Jack asked.

Wade shook his head. "Naw. I don't care to punch him and, frankly, I'll bet Olivia knows. I doubt if he could fool her. It's Dad I worry about the most. I'm not angry. Wynn solved a situation for me. I'm so relieved to have my memory back that I don't give a damn about what shenanigans he pulled.

"I didn't know I'd lose my memory, but I have it back now, so things should settle."

"Yeah, after Dad gets through blowing his lid over Wynn taking your identity."

"I'm remembering other times when he's done this, but he never involved the family in it."

"Yeah, he's never done it on this scale. You know he was actually on local television and all sorts of media as you?"

Wade nodded. "I'll get even with him someday."

Jack laughed. "I'm not holding my breath until that happens. He has a lot of luck and he has Mom's support."

When Wade heard the front door open and close, he said, "Let's go greet them." He walked out in time to catch up with Lucy.

"I want to see this," she said, falling into step with her brothers.

"It's just twins greeting each other, even if one

has been posing as the other. Frankly, I'm not angry about it. I hope Olivia is happy with him."

They entered the great room and Olivia turned to greet them. The smile on her face fell and she looked startled.

"Hello, Olivia. Good news. I've got my memory back."

Her eyes widened and for a moment he saw her surprise, but then it was gone and she smiled, looking composed and amused. "I'm glad. I must say you have an interesting brother. I'm enjoying getting to know him better."

"'Interesting' is one way to describe Wynn, I suppose. Where is he?"

"In the library waiting for you to join him."

"I wish you both the best."

"You sound as if you really mean that," she said, looking intently at him.

"I'm sincere or I wouldn't say it. I think you'll be good for Wynn. You won't let him get away with all the stuff he does now."

She smiled. "You mean that, don't you? I'm glad," she added without giving him time to answer her. "I think it was over between us, anyway. Wynn does entertain me. He can be fun and exciting."

"I'm sure that's true."

"I wish you the best and I'm glad you're safely home."

"Thanks, Olivia. Have fun with Wynn."

She smiled and nodded at him as he walked away.

His affair with her was over—and all he felt was relief.

The library doors were closed so he knocked, then stepped inside and closed the door for privacy. He faced his brother, who stood by the fireplace looking neat in navy slacks and a white dress shirt that was open at the throat—looking the way Wade dressed. "Well, we look like the ultimate identical twins tonight, right down to matching watches. You have on my boots," Wade said and saw Wynn turn to look at him sharply and frown.

"I'm home again and I have my memory back, Wynn," Wade stated bluntly.

"Ah, there go my plans for the evening." He stepped away from the fireplace, a drink in his hand. "So you know I've been impersonating you."

Wade nodded. He expected Wynn to look guilty, embarrassed, something. But no emotion showed on his face.

Wynn walked to him and sipped the amber liquid in his glass, nonchalant and at ease. "Olivia is a beautiful woman," he said, spearing Wade with an intent look. "She knew the truth right away, but played along, anyway."

"Yes, she is, and if that's why you did it, well, you succeeded. I wish you both well. Olivia and I were over, anyway, as she probably told you."

"No, she didn't and I don't think she actually knew you were over, but I'm glad." He put down his glass on a nearby table. "So you're not angry?" Wynn asked, tilting his head to again study his brother.

In all honesty, he should be. But he was so relieved to have his memory back that he couldn't muster the ire at Wynn's antics. Still, he stood firm. "No. But you can't pass as me now, so that's over. How did you know I wasn't on my way home when you came home?"

"I keep in touch with Mom and she chatters and tells me where everyone is and what's going on and I learned they'd lost contact with you. I saw a chance for some fun so I cut short my Nashville trip and flew home. I called on the way. Everyone accepted me as you. I didn't know how long before you'd surface."

"Your days of impersonating me are over."

"How very civilized. I figured you'd be furious. Dad will no doubt take his usual dim view."

"Something just occurred to me. The sheriff of the little town who saw you impersonate me on the news made arrangements for me to get the key to my condo when I got back to Dallas. I realize now I have the key to *your* condo." He looked down at himself. "And I'm wearing your clothes." He reached into his pocket, retrieved the keys and tossed them to Wynn.

"Keep the clothes," Wynn said. "I just got those and the ones I'm wearing because they look like what you'd wear. I don't want them back." He put the keys in his pocket. "It never occurred to me that the sheriff would arrange for you to pick up the keys to my condo."

"Don't worry, I didn't disturb anything," he said, knowing if the situation had been reversed, Wynn would have gone through every one of his things out of curiosity.

"I don't know how you can tolerate the damn boots. I'll be even happier when this whole charade is over with."

Wynn's bland expression hardened. His jawline tightened and his eyes narrowed as they assessed his twin.

"You know, Wade, you always think you're better than I am, that I can't have what you have. But I've proved you wrong with Olivia. You're not getting her back."

"I can live with that, Wynn," Wade said, maintaining his calm. "And I don't always think I'm better. We're just different."

"Not too different, my brother. You've got the same blood in your veins as I do in mine. And guess what? Mom told me the 'big secret'—" his hands formed air quotes "—that I'm not supposed to share with you or anybody else, but I think this is the right time to reveal it. Dad isn't our real dad," he said, lowering his voice. His face flushed and his voice deepened as he continued. "Ethan got Mom pregnant, which makes Dad our uncle. Guess we'll have to call him Uncle Arlo now, huh?"

The news hit Wade like a semitruck. "You're lying," he said, staring at his twin.

"Oh, no, I'm not. And our real dad didn't know it because Mom was just barely pregnant when Ethan was killed. At the time he died, neither of them knew she was pregnant and she's never told Arlo. So live with that one," he said as he snatched his drink and looked at Wade as he gulped it. "Our so-called dad doesn't even know he's not our father. You may be his favorite but you're not his son." He looked smug as he added, "And you won't tell because that might give him a heart attack, so I know you'll keep Mom's secret."

As the revelation rumbled around in his head, he thought of his mother and the relationship she and his twin shared. And he felt sick to his stomach, disgusted and angry. "The one person on earth who is always good to you no matter what you do and you didn't even give her the loyalty of keeping her secret."

"I know you won't say anything to her because you won't want to hurt her." He pointed a finger at Wade and added, "Now you can think about that one and whose blood runs in your veins."

Wade wanted to punch his brother but he wouldn't stoop to Wynn's level. He took deep breaths and jammed his fists into his pockets, calling up every ounce of self-control. When he couldn't contain his anger, he turned to go, to get away from Wynn. Walking to the door, he stopped.

He turned around to see Wynn smiling because he knew he had gotten to Wade.

He crossed the hall to speak to them. "He knows I have my memory. I'm going to call Dad and break the news to him before he walks in and gets it from Wynn without knowing how well I am."

"That's a good idea," Lucy said. "It won't worry Dad nearly as much if he thinks you're okay."

"And it'll help for him to talk to you," Jack added.

"I'll be outside," Wade said and left, going down the steps and away from the house. He was stunned by Wynn's news, but he didn't doubt it was the truth. His dad was his uncle Ethan, a man who had been just like Wynn. So he and Wynn had Ethan's blood in their veins and not the blood of Arlo Sterling, the man he called dad. Wade hoped his father never found out.

*Father.* What was he thinking? Arlo Sterling was their dad—in all ways except by blood. He had raised them, taken care of them, showered them with love and guidance and wealth. He would always be the real dad to Wade.

But he couldn't get the blood inheritance out of his mind. Wynn's words echoed there. *Now you can think about...whose blood runs in your veins.* That just fortified Wade's determination to never marry and have kids.

That made him think about Ava. They weren't talking marriage, but still, he needed to warn her that he was definitely not a marrying man. He recalled his conversation with Jack. How much was Wynn like their uncle Ethan because of blood—or was it because their mother had always spoiled him and thought whatever he did was cute?

Wade stood with clenched fists, gulping air, trying to calm down. He didn't want kids because they might be like Wynn. He couldn't risk it. But was he making a mistake?

Ava wanted four or five kids, she had said. He

thought about the odds on that. Four or five kids—if he married her and had five kids, two or three of them could be like Wynn. Hell, all five could be. What a thought.

As usual Wynn had once again stirred up trouble at a time when Wade had been happy and enjoying his homecoming. He had been filled with joy to have his memory back. He was even happy that Olivia and Wynn had found each other, and best of all, he had been filled with eagerness and joy because he would be with Ava later tonight. And then Wynn had thrown a damper on the evening. And broken a promise to their mother, but she would forgive him as she always did.

Wade stood outside in the dark, light spilling from the windows. As he called his dad, he again affirmed that Arlo would always be Dad to him. He listened to the phone ring and then heard his father's voice.

"Dad, I'm back and I'm fine. Good news—since I got home, my memory seems to have fully returned."

"Oh, son, that's great news." He could hear the relief in his father's voice.

"Look, we can talk more when you get home, but I'm so happy to be home and remember everything. I want you to know that I'm Wade. Wynn has been telling all of you that he was me." He listened to his father swear and hoped he hadn't made a mistake telling him on the phone.

"No one was hurt and I'm fine now that I'm home. Let it go because I'm okay and I don't want you to worry." The words nearly choked in his throat, but concern for his father made him force them out.

His father asked a few questions, his tone turning calmer with each of Wade's responses. "I think Wynn did it to get Olivia," Wade said, "and I'm glad because now she's happy and I don't have to go through breaking up with her."

His dad laughed. "I guess Wynn's good for something."

"Listen, Dad, I'm bringing a guest tonight. She got me out of that canyon and took me to her home. I can't wait for you and the family to meet her. But right now I better go back inside." Before he disconnected the call, he added, "I don't think I tell you often enough—you've been a super dad. I love you," he said and meant it. "See you soon."

He sighed, knowing that his father didn't deserve a son like Wynn. Which only made him more resolute in his decision never to marry and risk having a kid like his twin. He thought about Ava. At some point he needed to tell her how he felt. He didn't want to hurt her, but they'd been together only briefly. Surely both of them could walk away after only a few nights. Or was he fooling himself?

As quickly as that thought came, it was followed by another—he wasn't ready to say goodbye yet. He wanted her in his arms tonight, in his bed, and he wanted to kiss and make love for hours.

He looked at his watch and couldn't wait for her arrival. Twenty minutes later, Ava turned into the long circle drive and Wade went down the porch steps to meet her.

# Eight

Smiling at him, she stepped out of the car, looking like an angel, her silky blond hair framing her beautiful face. Her black dress almost covered her knees and the scoop neckline was not cut low enough to reveal her cleavage, but he knew every curve of her body intimately. She took his breath away just looking at her. He wanted to walk up to her, take her in his arms and kiss her.

Instead, he waited as she walked toward him. "You look fantastic. And I can't wait to get you home," he said in a husky voice.

"Thank you." Her smile broadened. "I can't tell you how thrilled I am that you remember your past life."

"You know what I remember most of all?" he said,

knowing his voice was deeper, something that happened when he was aroused.

"What?" she asked, looking up at him.

"Making love with you."

Her cheeks flushed. "I think we need to change the subject right now. Why don't you tell me the names of everyone I'm about to meet?"

While they walked to the house, he told her the names of his family. They went inside and he introduced her to everyone. He could see curiosity in Wynn's eyes, but his twin stayed at Olivia's side, merely giving Ava a curt wave. Lucy and Jack were happy to talk to Ava and hear about the storm and Wade's wreck. His mother stood talking to Wynn and Olivia. And then his dad arrived. He walked straight over to greet Wade, thrusting out his hand and then giving Wade a hug.

"Thank goodness, you're home," he said. "I've had business and wasn't home sometimes when Wynn was here as you. And the few times I was here with him, I just didn't pay attention. He's a good actor."

"Oh, yes. And he knows me well." Wade didn't want to talk about Wynn's charade. There was a more important reason to talk to his dad right now.

"I want you to meet Ava," Wade said, taking his dad's arm and crossing the room to where she stood with Lucy and Jack. "Dad, meet Ava Carter. She came to my rescue and I think she saved my life. Ava, this is my dad, Arlo Sterling."

"Mr. Sterling, I'm so happy to meet you. And I think Wade would have survived on his own, but I'm sure he had a better stay in my place out of the storm," she said, smiling at his father and offering her hand.

"I'm sure he did, too, Ava, and we're all grateful to you for what you did to take care of him."

As they stood talking, Wade studied his dad and realized he didn't look as good as he had only a couple of days ago. He wondered how much Wynn's constant annoyances had hurt their dad's health. His attention shifted to Ava and he wanted dinner to be over and for them to be able to go. He wanted her all to himself and it seemed far longer than just earlier today that they had last been together.

By the time dinner was over and they had visited for an hour, Wade felt they could leave. Goodbyes took time and finally he walked to Ava's car with her. She slid behind the wheel to drive.

"I keep extra keys in my dad's safe, locked away from Wynn," Wade said when he was in the car. "So now I have my condo key and my car keys. The pickup that went into the canyon was one of my ranch vehicles. Let's go to my place. That way I can get my car and I can entertain you."

"Sounds like a deal. I can't wait for you to entertain me," she said in a sultry voice, her eyes on the road.

"You shouldn't do that when you're driving because answers like that, said the way you did, tend to cause me to want to put my hands on you and kiss you and I can't while you drive."

"That'll just make you look forward to being home with me again," she answered.

"Ava, I've been looking forward to getting home again with you since I stepped out of your car this afternoon. You can't imagine how much I've thought about you since then."

"We better change the drift of this conversation because I need to keep my attention on the road. You're definitely distracting."

"And you are definitely sexy and hot."

Ava glanced his way for a second, then averted her eyes back to the road and sat up straighter. "You have a nice big family. Four kids is wonderful."

"Three of us are and you're changing the subject."

She laughed. "Oh, yes, I am before I throw myself in your arms and wreck the car."

"Next time, let me drive. I've developed the knack of driving and talking at the same time," he answered, amused, excited to be with her and aware his condo was closer than her house. He couldn't wait to get there.

"What part of what I said do you not get?"

He smirked, though he knew she couldn't see it. "I can't help it. You *are* sexy and hot."

"Stop," she said, smiling, but keeping her attention on the road ahead and city traffic. "How many more blocks to your place?"

"About another couple of miles. Want me to drive?"

"No, I don't. Your twin seemed charming tonight."

"Oh, he can be, especially to a beautiful, sexy woman. He can turn it on whenever he wants. He keeps on Mom's good side and she adores him. Believe me, you'll always see his good side."

"I've seen identical twins before and I could tell them apart, but I can't with the two of you. I can see how he gets away impersonating you—except you have a scar on your left hand."

"Didn't you see a band aid on his hand?"

"Yes, I did. I figured he cut himself."

"And that's what he would tell you, but underneath that band aid is no cut and no scar. He wears that so women who know me and know I have the scar think he has a cut where the scar is. He's devious and he's an actor. In high school he constantly passed himself off as me with girls I dated and only a few of them ever caught on. But he won't be able to do it so easily anymore."

"Why is that?" she asked.

"If you ever wonder if you're really with me, ask to look at my shoulder. Molly said I'm going to have a scar. And Wynn isn't going to be able to do anything to match the way I've got my shoulder scarred."

"I'll keep that in mind," she teased him.

Wade continued looking out the window. "I recognize everything. Molly was right. My memory came back and it seems to be all there. All this is familiar like I never had a problem."

"I'm glad."

He turned to gaze at her. "Best of all, I can fully remember last night with you."

"I'm not even going to answer that and then you'll have to stop."

"That's okay if you don't join in my conversation.

I'll just tell you about last night and how we showered together and—"

"If I wreck the car, you'll be sorry."

He laughed, enjoying teasing her and talking about sex. "You won't wreck the car. You're concentrating while I'm remembering the moments, holding you, kissing you—"

She began to sing softly and he laughed. Then he remained quiet because they were almost to his condo, six blocks off the busy highway.

He had a private entrance and the minute the door closed behind them, he turned to wrap his arms around her. He looked into her big blue eyes and felt his heartbeat race. "Finally, you're here and I can kiss you," he whispered. "I've waited forever for this moment."

Ava shivered as his gaze held hers and she could see his intent in his expression. She shrugged the strap to her purse off her shoulder and let it fall to the floor. There was only the soft light in the entryway, but she was oblivious of everything except Wade, who looked so incredibly handsome tonight.

Her heart pounded in eager anticipation as she wrapped her arms around him and kissed him in return, forgetting everything else.

He crushed her against him, kissing her passionately. She trembled with wanting him, feeling as much urgency as he seemed to feel. As he kissed her, his hands were at the zipper of her dress, slipping the zipper slowly down the back.

He raised his head for a moment and pushed away her dress. It fell in a heap around her feet. His muscled chest expanded as he took a deep breath, placed his hands on her waist and took a step back to look at her. While his gaze ran over her, she tingled with the need to kiss him again. "Wade," she whispered, tugging his forearms lightly.

Instead of reaching for her, he undid two buttons on his shirt and yanked it over his head to toss it aside.

Then he turned his attention to her remaining clothing. He unfastened her bra and dropped it. "You're beautiful," he whispered as he pushed down her lacy panties so she could step out of them.

After he shed his slacks and shorts, he sheathed himself with a condom and walked back into her embrace, and she could feel his thick manhood, hard and ready, pressing against her.

"I've thought about you constantly," he whispered between showering kisses on her throat and down to take first one nipple and then the other in his mouth. He ran his tongue over her and teased her with slow, wet strokes, his warm breath on her while he cupped her breasts in his gentle hands.

She gasped while each stroke of his fingers heightened her desire.Urgency built to make love, to have him fill her, to love her until she felt she would burst with her climax as only he could bring her to.

With a cry, she brought his head up. The desire she saw in his brown eyes made her stand on tiptoe and kiss him while she caressed his manhood.

When he picked her up, she locked her legs around him as he let her down slowly and entered her.

She gasped with an aching need for his loving.

As they kissed, he pumped hard and fast while she moved on him and held him tightly. Longing built, driving her. He went harder and faster while she clung to him and finally cried out with her climax, consumed by bliss. He thrust one more time and followed her into ecstasy.

When she finally lowered her feet to the floor, she was grateful for his embrace because her legs felt too weak to support her. Perhaps sensing it, he swept her up in his arms.

He carried her to his shower, switching on lights as he went. Unaware of her surroundings, she could see only him as he gazed down at her while he carried her through his condo. Basking in the afterglow of the orgasm he'd given her, she showered light kisses on his throat and his ear, as her hand played across his nape and she wound her fingers in his thick hair. He was a marvel to her, their lovemaking carrying her to heights she had never been.

"Sexy man, so, so sexy," she whispered.

He stopped walking, turning his head to kiss her passionately again while he held her tightly against him. Finally he raised his head and continued into a large bathroom with a king-size shower. As they showered together, she ran her hands over his exciting body. They dried each other with thick, fluffy red towels, then once again he picked her up and carried her into his bedroom.

In minutes they were in each other's arms in the bed with a sheet pulled over them and a low light on a table beside them.

"Ava, I've thought about you constantly since the last time we made love. You're special," he said, showering feathery kisses on her face. He leaned away to look at her. "I don't want to ever hurt you." She shifted so they were facing each other and he toyed with her hair, his brown eyes intent on her.

"You won't hurt me," she said, certain he wouldn't. He had been considerate of her feelings since the first time they were together.

With his fingers he combed long strands of her hair from her face and gazed at her seriously. "Ava, I want to tell you something right now. You've been hurt badly by your ex-fiancé. I don't want to add another hurt."

Suddenly Ava felt chilled and wondered what was coming because he looked solemn. Whatever it was, he probably hadn't remembered it until he got back to Dallas, to his home, and his memory returned. It couldn't be a wife, so she was puzzled, but she had a feeling that it wasn't going to be good news. He looked far too worried.

"You should realize now at least to a degree what my twin is like. He has made my dad's life miserable too many times. Dad has heart trouble and I told you that when he was fifty-two, he had a stroke. I blame Wynn for the worries our dad has had. Wynn made Jack's life miserable when he was a little kid, and he was mean to Lucy. He did stuff to me, too, but I'm his age and could beat him in a fight when we were kids. But he didn't stop when we grew up, posing as me, like he did now. I was going out with Olivia until I left for the fishing trip. I was planning to break it off with her, so I'm glad she's happy with him, but if I'd been in love with her, I would be livid with him now."

"I would think she would be because of his deception."

"Oh, no. He can be charming and she was through with me, too. Wynn got what he wanted—Olivia. That was the whole purpose of this switch."

"I understand, Wade. I know you have no feelings for Oliva. If that's what you're trying to tell me—"

"No, Ava, there's more." He took a deep breath and when she saw the darkness shield his eyes, she braced for the bad news.

# Nine

"What I'm working up to tell you is, because of my brother, I have never wanted to marry and I sure never want to have kids."

"Wade, you're not like your brother, and a child you raise wouldn't be like him. Your brother wouldn't have any great influence on your child."

"Influence matters, but genes—you have to live with them and you can't change some things that you inherit."

"You don't inherit a mean disposition when you're around nice people all the time."

"I'm very much like my dad who raised me," Wade said. "Wynn isn't like him one bit. We had the same dad raise us. We have the same blood in our veins, but there are qualities Wynn has that I don't have and vice-versa."

"Wade, you're cutting yourself off from so much joy. Family is everything. You have a brother and sister and parents that you like, right?"

"Yes, I do, but I've watched Wynn ruin my dad's health by simply worrying him constantly when we were growing up. He still does, for that matter. Look at this latest escapade."

"I don't think you're looking at the positive things. I'm alone. You have no idea what it's like to have no family. And you have a good family—all the other members. Lucy and Jack are friendly and nice. Your parents are warm. And Wynn—well, he's not a monster, Wade. I know he causes the family trouble, but he isn't dangerous. You seem to deal pretty well with him. And I don't think any child you'd raise would ever be like him. I don't think his jealousy, or whatever motivates him, is something a child of yours would inherit. You don't inherit jealousy."

Wade shook his head. "You don't know the whole story. We have two personalities that are alike in different generations."

"I'm not following you."

"It isn't just Wynn, Ava. My dad had a younger brother, Ethan. My parents and my older relatives have always said that Wynn is just like Ethan. So there's one like that in that generation and one in mine. Ethan and Wynn had different parents, different siblings, different influences in their lives, but they turned out the same way. I don't want to go through what my dad did raising Wynn. My grand-father had heart trouble and he died at sixty-three. I don't know if Ethan contributed to his health prob-lems or not. I just told this to Jack today and he said he feels the same way."

"I can't imagine that you would have a child who would be like your brother. I think you're worrying unnecessarily."

"I might be, Ava, but I'm sticking by that, so I wanted you to know right now. I'm not a marrying man and I don't want kids. I'm not going to change."

Ava felt as if ice water had been poured over her as she listened to his declaration about marriage and kids. Then she tried reasoning it out. She thought how little time they had been together and what a short time she had known him. They weren't in love. This was lust and she knew that.

She looked into his eyes. They were in bed to-gether, naked, they had made love, he was exciting, irresistible, handsome, sexy. Tonight she wasn't going to worry about his determination to stay single all his life and to avoid having kids. Tonight that wasn't a problem. Because she knew they couldn't be in love in this short amount of time.

She knew something else, too. Their relationship would have to be brief or she would be in love with him.

She wanted to make love, wanted his kisses, but she would have to guard her heart and tell him good-bye very soon. The realization hurt, but the pain would be easier to bear in the short term. Wade was a wonderful, sexy man, but she had dreams for a family and he would never give her that.

Sadness replaced the trepidation she felt when he'd started talking to her. "That's unfortunate for you, Wade, because you'd be a wonderful husband and dad. I can't imagine you'd have a son like your twin or your uncle. You're cutting yourself out of a family and children and to my way of thinking that's one of the biggest joys in life."

He lowered his gaze for a moment, then looked back at her. This time, his eyes shone with desire. "At the moment, I can think of another huge joy in life and we're letting it slip away from us," he said, starting to nuzzle her neck and then trail kisses on her ear.

His touch was like a balm. It turned her sadness and pain to longing and arousal. She met his kiss and felt that familiar yearning for his lovemaking. Tonight she wasn't going to think about his views of marriage and children. She wasn't in love and he wasn't in love, and she was certain she could still tell him goodbye without being hurt. She let him kiss away all thoughts and even the worries he had just caused. For this night she would be in his arms.

She held him, running her hand over his smooth, muscled back and giving herself to his fiery loving. This time, words were nonexistent—everything was erotic feelings, with his hands and mouth all over her. She rubbed against him, kissed and stroked him with her hands and tongue, making him groan with desire. It seemed he'd never stop teasing and toying with her, never give her all of himself, which her body craved.

Then, finally he had a condom and was on his back as he lifted her over him and she slid down for him to enter her. She cried out with pleasure, setting the pace as she rocked against him, then moving faster, as he caressed her breasts and pumped in her.

They climaxed together, his arms around her, with her sprawled over him, holding him tightly.

She didn't know how long her explosive climax rocked her, but finally she slowed and then lay quietly on him, his arm around her while his other hand caressed her back, sliding over her bottom, her thighs and up again.

"So perfect," he whispered, "so beautiful." He kissed her lightly. "So sexy. This night is a dream come true."

She held him, her ear against his chest, and she heard his pounding heart slow and finally reach a normal beat, and her breathing matched his.

At this moment, in his bed, in his embrace, lying on top of him, their warm, naked bodies together after fantastic sex, she tingled everywhere from his loving and she was satiated. At this minute, with him, there were no problems.

But with each calmer breath, the world, their lives and concerns and dreams, all began to come back. She heard his heartbeat, remembering his words. *I'm not a marrying man and I don't want kids. I'm not going to change.*

She chased the worry away. She hadn't known him long and they weren't in love. She could get over him.

All they had between them were hours at her cabin and a few intimate moments.

Or was she kidding herself? Was she taking a big risk with her heart again to be with him?

She shifted to her side and slid off of him. He left for a few minutes to rid himself of the condom and returned to stretch out beside her. Drawing her tightly against his side, he held her close while she tangled her fingers in the thick mat of curly, black hair across his chest.

Each time she started to think about what he had told her, she tried to shut it out of her mind and focus on his body and the loving they'd already shared. There would be time later to think more clearly about his declarations of no marriage and no family.

"A kiss for your thoughts. I don't exactly have a penny with me," he said.

"I was thinking how sexy you are," she said in a lazy drawl. Tonight she was in his arms and she wanted to make love until dawn. She brushed kisses across his shoulder to his throat, then he shifted beneath her and his mouth covered hers in a hungry kiss.

He held her close. "Go to dinner with me tomorrow night, Ava. You took care of me after getting me out of the canyon and I want to take you out."

"Thank you, that's very nice," she said. Then caution reared its head, a warning light in the darkness, making her question the wisdom of continuing to see him. Dinner would no doubt lead to more lovemaking afterward and that would just put another link in an invisible chain that could bind her heart to him. Only he would never love her in return. She heard the firmness in his voice when he told her he didn't want to marry and he never wanted kids.

She did and she was certain she could never stay with a man who didn't want children.

It was just dinner, another part of her brain reasoned. A chance for Wade to show his gratitude for her kindness and hospitality. And didn't she owe him a note of thanks, too? Because of him, she was over her heartbreak with Judd.

She should be able to recover from whatever hurt she would feel when she and Wade parted later. Compared to the time she had spent with her ex-fiancé, she had barely been with Wade.

His arm tightened around her and his dark eyes searched hers. "What are you thinking? Will you go to dinner with me?"

Her mouth opened, her response surprising her. "Yes, I will. I need to go home first. I have calls, mail, things I should do. I'll be happy to go to dinner tomorrow, thank you."

"Good," he said, smiling at her. He kissed her lightly, wrapped her in his arms and held her. "Ava, I've seen your cabin, where you like to spend time and relax. I'd like to show you my ranch. We don't have to stay long. I just want to show you what I love and where I work. Will you go to my ranch with me?"

For a moment she thought about it. That would be more time with him, getting to know him better and seeing another part of his life. Did she want that risk to her heart?

"I'll have to think about that one," she said.

"I want you to see it," he said. "I haven't ever asked any other woman out to the ranch. You're very special," he whispered, showering light kisses on her throat and then down to her breasts. She wound her fingers in his hair, and all thoughts ceased as she was swept away by his tongue, his kisses and his hands on her.

It was noon when, showered and dressed, she walked into the living room to find him.

"I need to go home, get my mail and calls, do some things."

"Let's go to lunch and then you go," he said and she nodded. "And before we go to lunch, I'd like to take you with me tomorrow. My cousin Jake Reed called. My cousins and I donated money to build a new arena in Fort Worth this past year."

"That was in all the news," she said.

"My cousins and I haven't seen the building—they haven't seen it since the ground-breaking ceremony. I've seen it, but not recently and when I saw it, it was spectacular. Anyway, we have an arena board now and an arena CEO and other employees. We've been invited to come look at the arena. We're going to meet in the morning and tour, look at it. I'd like you to go with me."

She smiled. "I'd love to. I've heard so much about it on television. I'd love to go."

"Great," he said, laughing slightly. "I was in hopes when you said you'd love to go that you would add that you would love to be with me."

She laughed and rushed up to put her arms around his neck. "Of course, I'd love to go mainly to be with you," she said. They looked into each other's eyes and laughed and then the moment changed. Her heartbeat speeded and she tightened her arms around his neck and stood on tiptoe as he wrapped his arms around her waist, drew her to him while he leaned down to kiss her.

They had lunch together and he went to her car with her.

"I'll pick you up at half past six," he told her through her open window. "I have your address. I don't even want to tell you goodbye and let you go now."

She smiled at him. "I'll see you tonight."

He nodded and stepped away from the car. When she reached the corner, she glanced in the rearview mirror to see he was still standing, watching her.

"I shouldn't go out with you tonight or tomorrow or ever again," she whispered to herself. His announcement about never marrying and never having children came crashing back now, and this time she had to face the truth of what he had told her and how it affected their relationship. She should have said goodbye when she left, but she couldn't resist him.

It hurt to know a parting would come, and she feared that this one would be a whole lot worse than the first one.

* * *

In his jeans, red, white and blue plaid shirt and boots, Wade stepped out of his car. Lucy had asked him and Jack to look at her new house. She stood outside waiting and smiled when he was close, then hugged him lightly. "Thanks for coming to see my new home."

"Wouldn't miss seeing it," he said and turned to shake hands with Jack. "I'm glad you're here."

"I didn't invite Wynn and probably never will," she said. "Sorry. If I do, it'll be because of Olivia. I do like her."

"Don't apologize. Wynn caused you to feel that way. But I'm telling you, Olivia may bring about some changes for the better in our brother," Wade remarked and Lucy rolled her eyes.

"I'll believe that when I see it. I hear you're not coming to the family dinner tonight," she said as they walked to the front door of her house.

"No. I had already asked Ava to go to dinner with me and I'm not joining the family instead, even if she is also invited, which she was."

"I don't know whether Wynn will really care or not. He does love an audience and I happen to know from someone else that he gave Olivia a huge diamond engagement ring last night and she accepted his offer of marriage. Can you imagine Wynn married?" Lucy asked, laughing while Jack shook his head.

"He's in love, believe it or not—the guy must be able to love someone besides himself," Jack said.

"Well, I know Olivia," Wade told them. "Our

brother's met his match in her. Just watch. I predict you're not going to recognize Wynn. He will not be impersonating me ever again and I would bet the ranch on it."

"Wow," Lucy said, staring at Wade. "She can influence him that much? I can't imagine he wanted to marry her if she'll be calling the shots."

"She's perfect for him. She has old money. She's gorgeous. She can be fun. He'll find out what a strong, smart woman he married. I don't think he'll ever regret it, either. She'll keep him happy, but it'll be on her terms."

"Well, that is the best news possible," Lucy said. "I'm really impressed and I hope with all my heart you know what you're talking about. Our whole family will be happier if that's true about Olivia."

"Oh, damn right," Jack said. "That's fantastic news." He gave a whoop and laughed. "Ah, someone to finally boss Wynn. Even Dad couldn't."

"You watch how he changes," Wade said. "She has more money in her family than we do in ours and that will make Wynn think twice about crossing her. Trust me. I know Olivia. Believe me, our brother has met his match." He turned and looked at the front door of the house. "Well, let's see your new home, Luce." He stepped behind her as she unlocked the door and stepped inside.

The entryway opened into a great room that had a huge wood-burning fireplace, two walls of glass that overlooked a small yard, and beyond the backyard was a country-club golf course.

"Good view without having your own big yard," Wade remarked.

"I like your contemporary furniture," Jack added. Wade looked at the room. It was painted in a light shade, the furniture modern with open spaces and a polished hardwood floor. "Very nice," he said. He thought about what it would be like to have his own house with Ava and the idea held appeal.

"I like it and it should be relatively easy to care for," Wade said.

They looked at her office, which had a glass-and-metal desk, built-in file cabinets, a long glass table.

She showed them two bedroom suites and a third bedroom, a contemporary kitchen with floor-to-ceiling glass along one wall and light spilling into the room.

Finally she locked up as they left. "Thanks, guys, for your interest."

Wade hugged her lightly. "I'm glad to see your new home and I'm glad, too, that you're doing so well in the real-estate business. You're a young broker."

"I love it and because of my family, I have lots of good contacts."

"Have fun tonight," Wade said. "Both of you. And welcome Olivia into the family for me. I've already called her and told her I was sorry I wouldn't be there for dinner. She seems truly happy and she'll be a great addition to the family."

"I hope Wynn has half a dozen kids and they're all like him," Jack said and then shrugged. "Well, maybe not if Olivia is a nice person. I wouldn't wish that on her." He let out a laugh. "This is one wedding I'm looking forward to. Hot dog!"

Wade laughed. "I'll second that." But as he drove away, all his thoughts shifted from his twin to Ava. He couldn't wait for tonight.

Excitement bubbled in Ava as she studied herself in the mirror. Her hair was parted in the center and fell straight on either side of her face. She wore a black sleeveless dinner dress with a deep V-neckline that revealed her curves, the skirt coming to midcalf. She wore high-heeled black pumps that showcased her legs and a diamond bracelet that echoed the small stones lining the neckline of her dress.

She was so eager for this evening with Wade that she nearly jumped when she heard a car door shut. She looked out the window to see Wade striding toward the house. In a charcoal Western-cut suit, a white dress shirt, gold cuff links in the French cuffs and black boots, he took her breath away. The breeze caught locks of his midnight hair and lifted a curl off his forehead. His injuries had healed and he was incredibly good-looking.

She wanted to run out and throw herself into his arms and kiss him while he carried her to bed. She also wanted an evening out with him because she had fun with him. It was exciting to be with him and she could look forward to coming back to share the rest of the night. She glanced around her house and her bedroom. She only had two bedrooms. Wade didn't seem to care what she had or didn't have. Then she forgot all about the house and furniture. Tomorrow she had already told him she would go with him to look at the new arena in Ft. Worth. She wanted to do that.

So for now, she simply wasn't going to worry about the future or telling him goodbye. She was just going to enjoy being with him and hope she could hang on to her heart enough that she wouldn't be deeply in love with him.

He was the best-looking man she had ever known, she thought again as she rushed to open the door.

When she did, he had started to reach to ring the bell. Instead, he just wrapped his arm around her waist, stepped inside and closed the door behind them. He kissed her, an all-consuming kiss that made her feel as if she would melt in his arms.

Finally, he released her. "I promised you dinner and that's what we're going to do." Still, he didn't move toward the door, instead taking her in from head to toe. "You look gorgeous. You can eat and I'll watch you."

She laughed. "Don't be ridiculous."

"Come on. If we don't go now, we never will."

He took her hand and opened the front door. She set the alarm, picked up her small black purse and closed the door behind them, hearing the lock click.

He took her to a downtown private dinner club and she had a delicious steak dinner, but she could barely eat because all she could do was think about kissing him and making love again.

It would be a bittersweet night, but she wanted more time with him. And she couldn't keep telling herself it would only be one more time. Soon she knew she had to say goodbye and mean it or she might fall deeply in love with him. She would worry about that in another few days.

The early morning sun was bright in Fort Worth, the air crisp with a fresh smell. The city was still relatively quiet even though work-day traffic was picking up. She wore a frilly blue blouse, jeans and sandals and had her blond hair tied behind her head with a narrow blue silk scarf. She was happy to be with Wade, eager to see the arena.

When Wade and Ava drove into the Fort Worth parking lot there were already two pickups there. Two men stood talking, until he came into view and then they stopped talking and turned to watch him drive up beside their pickups. Dressed the same as he was, both had broad-brimmed hats, one gray hat and one black. Both men wore cowboy boots. They had on jeans and Western style long-sleeved cotton shirts.

"Are they your cousins?" she asked, certain they were.

"Yes, they are. Jake and Luke. I have other cousins, too."

"I feel like I shouldn't be here," Ava said. "I'll be the only woman here."

"Believe me, every man here will be glad you're here. Watch them try to get close to talk to you. It'll be nice for them to get to see the arena we donated money to build, but believe me, they will be more interested in talking to you. Luke, maybe just being polite."

"He's the one you said lost his family two years ago when his wife and baby were killed in a car wreck."

"Yep. He hasn't been the same since."

"I guess not. You couldn't ever get over that. That kind of loss makes a lot of other losses look insignificant. I'm surprised he can even get out of the house or that he wants to."

"You have to keep on living," Wade said. "Luke's a great guy. He's gotten very quiet, but you'll like him."

"I still don't think I should be here. This is a guy thing."

"No, it's not and we'll all enjoy your company and I'll do something special tonight to show you my appreciation that you came with me this morning. Believe me, I like it a thousand times better with you along." His gaze swept over her and she tingled as he smiled. After Wade parked, he grabbed his tan Stetson, put it on and stepped out to go around and open her door, taking her hand when she stepped down. She was aware of his warm hand closing lightly around hers. He looked handsome, strong and so appealing. He wore a navy shirt, jeans and boots. She was excited to be with him. She did feel slightly out of place, but she wanted to be with Wade and she wanted to see the arena. She knew it was a big thing for the city and the state and had cost millions, all donated by Wade and three of his cousins.

He extended his hand when he approached his cousins.

"Jake, it's good to see you," Wade said, shaking the hand of a man as tall as he was. They smiled as they shook.

"We were wondering when you were going to get here," Jake Reed kidded and they both laughed.

Wade turned to the other man and they shook hands. "Luke, it's good to see you. How're you doing?" he asked, looking intently at his cousin.

"Ava, I want you to meet my cousins. Cousins, meet Ava Carter. Ava, this is Jake Reed." He paused while Jake shook her hand and said hello.

"Ava, this is Luke Grayson. Luke meet Ava."

"I'm happy to meet you, Ava," Luke said, smiling warmly. "I'm glad you're with us this morning."

"Thank you," she said, smiling at Luke. "I'm glad to be here and get to see this new arena I've heard so much about. It'll be fantastic for the city and for the state."

"We hope so. The old arena was. We should get the grand tour," Luke said. He glanced at Wade. "How's Wynn?"

"Actually, maybe some slight changes. I think he'll stop impersonating me so that will be a relief." Wade glanced at Jake. "Jake, are you still fighting with your neighbor? Has either one of you taken the other to court this month?"

Jake shook his head. "Nope. We've had about eight months without a lawsuit or a big hassle. At least we don't shoot at each other like we've always been told the early day Reeds and Blakes did." As they all laughed, Ava was still looking over the new building.

"The facility looks wonderful from here," Ava stated and they all turned to look at the massive new building in a rich dark brown wood with glass along the center front running up to the roof. The first floor was the dark brown wood, but the upper floors had lots of glass to let in light.

"You'll like this arena," Wade said. He smiled at his cousins. "You two need to come to town more often and get off your ranches."

"As if you hang around Ft. Worth or Dallas," Jake drawled.

"It looks mighty good from out here," Luke said. "Course it should for what it cost."

"It's going to be great. It seats 11,360, there are 356 horse stalls. The building has a full service bar and an upper level cantina with catering," Wade said. "Our man, Bart Kingston will be here and he will tell you all about it," Wade said.

"You guys have seen it," Luke said. "It looks good from out here."

A black car turned into the lot and Wade paused. "Here comes Kingston. He's full of enthusiasm about this new arena. I think the arena board hired a very good guy for the job."

A tall, thin man with curly blond hair waved, parked and stepped out, hurrying toward them.

"Good morning. I got tied up in traffic held up by a train. It's good to see you," he said, extending his hand to shake hands with Wade.

"This is my friend, Ava Carter," Wade said as Bart Kingston shook hands with Jake.

"Ava, this is Bart Kingston who will be in charge of this arena."

Wade turned slightly. "Bart, this is my cousin, Luke Grayson and another cousin, Jake Reed."

"I'm so glad to meet you both and thank you in person for your magnificent, generous donations that made this arena possible," he said as he shook hands with Luke and Jake. He smiled at all three men. "All of you, I want to thank you again for your very generous donations to build this new arena. It is a fabulous building and we are already booked for wonderful horse shows and events. It's a boon to Texas and to the city. Let's go look at it. You're in for a great tour."

"I'm looking forward to seeing the arena. I've heard about it," Luke said.

"Miss Carter, I'm glad you could join us. Let me lead the way and unlock the place." He headed for the massive front doors with carved horses in the wood. As he walked, he talked.

"We'll have the U.S. West Finals Rodeo this year. We've booked an Arabian horse show, an Appaloosa horse show, a Morgan show and Quarter horses. This is going to be big on horses. We have three rodeos booked. We'll have a National Teen Championship Rodeo this year." He paused to unlock big double doors. Luke, Jake and Wade all stepped forward to open the massive doors. Wade took Ava's arm lightly and she stepped inside a huge entry area with marble columns and a gleaming hardwood floor. She noticed an inviting faint smell of new wood.

"This is beautiful," she told Wade.

"It's great, but the big deal is the arena floor and the horse accommodations—their stalls, the facilities for taking care of them. There are cattle pens and a big barn behind this building even though we're in town," Bart said. "Just follow me. I hope you're already enjoying the first part of our tour," he said to Ava, who smiled as she nodded.

"I'm enjoying it very much. This is a fantastic building."

"We think so," Bart said. "It's beautiful, and it's going to be even more so when we get the paintings up and a few more things done. Now here is the arena." He led them out into the center of the arena and it was dazzling to her as she looked around.

"I don't know anything about what should be here, but this looks fabulous," she told Wade.

"It is fabulous," he said while she looked at all the box seats that looked luxurious and roomy with comfortable big cushioned chairs, tables to hold food. Beyond the box seats were cushioned seats that had ample leg room and wide aisles.

"The sound will be excellent," Bart said. He turned to point up. "We have a cantina with a full service bar, a seating capacity of 260, we have six concession stands in the building."

Wade stood beside her on her left and Jake was to her right. Jake looked over her head at Wade. "Looks like they spent the money well. This is going to be a great arena. Almost makes me wish I still was signed up for bull riding. Almost. I'm smart enough to know my limits."

"I agree," Wade answered as they looked around.

"Do you like rodeos or horse shows?" Jake asked Ava.

"Rodeos. I've never seen a horse show."

"What's your profession, Ava?" he asked.

"I'm an occupational therapist and I work for my-self, so I have what I want to do. I provide home care," she told him and he nodded.

Bart motioned to them to follow him as he contin-ued talking while he moved on.

It was over an hour before they were through and had thanked Bart and finished talking to him. Wade held her arm lightly as they walked out with his cousins.

"It's going to be a great arena," Luke said.

"Yes, it is and we do have to pick a date for the grand opening, but the Board is going over the sched-ule and they have some new events to add, so we can't really get a date any time soon and we'll have to wait until Bart contacts us," Wade said and his cousins nodded.

"They still have to get their sign up with the arena name," Jake added. "It's going to be good when it's all ready. The Cal Brand Arena," he said. "The name is nice, but we'd all rather have Cal with us."

"Come go to lunch with us," Wade said.

"If Ava is going," Jake said, smiling at her and she smiled as she nodded.

"Yes, I am."

The cousins joined them and Ava found them to be fun and they were fun and happy being together. She felt a pang as she listened to them talk. Wade was so wonderful. The more she knew him, the more in love with him she was and it hurt. How could he not want his own children. He had wonderful cousins and they all had fun together. His children might be like his cousins instead of like his twin. Even though she heard what they were saying and laughed with them, she couldn't keep from thinking about Jake and how it was going to hurt to part with him. She had to do it and she knew it was going to break her heart. Today had just made her fall more deeply in love with Wade and his family.

She forced those thoughts out of her mind and then that evening when she was out with him, she had to try to bank the hurtful thoughts again. She enjoyed every moment of the wonderful dinner with him and every moment at his condo later and passionate, wild lovemaking all through the night and again in the morning.

When she woke, he wasn't beside her in the bed. But his scent lingered. She turned over and buried her face in his pillow, inhaling deeply and committing the scent to memory. Waking this morning, she knew what she had to tell Wade. And she knew that was their last night together.

Forcing herself out of bed, she showered and dressed in her black dress, the only clothes she had, and found him waiting in the kitchen with breakfast ready. Freshly showered, with damp hair, he was in jeans, a blue denim shirt and boots and he looked fantastic.

He walked up to kiss her, a long, sexy kiss that

made her weak in the knees and wanting to hold back the words she knew she needed to say to him.

When she looked into his eyes, she saw him tilt his head slightly, a questioning expression on his face. She wondered if he knew what she had to say. But in a flash, his face changed and he pulled her close again. "You look gorgeous," he said, kissing her.

He'd fixed a delicious-looking breakfast of eggs, toast, strawberries, blueberries and hot coffee, but she couldn't eat more than a few bites. It was too difficult to get food down her tight throat.

He sat back. "I'd like to show you my ranch today. Will you go with me?"

She gazed at him and with all her heart she wanted to say yes. Telling her he had never asked a woman to the ranch before meant she was special to him. But was she special enough to change his views of life and his determination to stay single and childless?

She knew she should resist the invitation. But how could she when he had as much as said that she was more important to him than any other woman in his past? Yet they had no future unless he changed.

She argued with herself to go and take that chance on him changing. As she mulled it over, his new cell phone chimed. She knew he had bought a new phone to replace the one he lost in the flood. He answered, frowned and got up from the table to cross the kitchen. He spoke softly and she didn't care to eavesdrop, but she couldn't keep from hearing a few words and the concern-filled tone of his voice.

When the call ended, he turned back to her. One look at his face and she knew it was bad news.

# Ten

"That was my brother Jack. Dad's in the hospital. They are putting in a pacemaker."

"Oh, Wade, I'm so sorry. I'll get a cab to get home. You go now to the hospital."

"No, I'll take you home, but I do want to go to the hospital now."

"Of course. But please let me call a cab."

He shook his head. "No. Your place is not out of the way," he said, raking his fingers through his damp hair.

"I'll get my purse," she said, rushing from the room, saying a silent prayer for Wade, his dad and his family. She hurt for Wade because it was obvious he was worried.

In minutes they were in the car and they made the

drive in silence. At her house when he pulled up in the drive, she turned to him as she unbuckled her seatbelt. "Don't get out. Let me out and you go. Call me later, please, and let me know how he is. Call me if I can do anything. You and your family are in my prayers."

He smiled at her. "Thanks. I'll get back to you when I see how Dad is."

She stepped out quickly and walked to her front door as she heard him drive away. At the porch steps she looked over her shoulder to see his car disappear around the corner and she couldn't help the feeling that he was driving out of her life.

This heart attack would reaffirm his feelings on marriage and children, no doubt because he'd attribute it to the anxiety caused his dad by Wynn's antics. Wade would be far more determined than ever now to never marry, never have children. Sadness and hurt filled her.

No matter how much he wanted her to, she couldn't go to his ranch with him. She couldn't go out again with him. It was time to walk out of his life forever.

The pain was monumental, far worse than she thought it would be.

It was about two hours later when she had a call from him.

"Sorry to take you home so abruptly. My dad is doing okay so far and it wasn't as bad as the family thought at first. They've installed a pacemaker and said he will be here tomorrow for certain and then they'll see how he is. He's done well, thank heavens."

Judging by how quickly the words tumbled from his lips, she knew he was stressed. And rightly so. She knew how much he loved his father. Before she had a chance to say anything, he asked her, "Will you go to dinner with me tonight? Nothing fancy, just go eat and be together. I don't want to be alone and I need to see you."

Her heart beat faster. She was hoping she didn't have to do this tonight, when he was so anxious about his father, but it couldn't go on. She had to say goodbye. "Yes, I will," she said, hurting for him, and for herself, knowing what was ahead.

"Good. How's seven?"

"Seven is fine. Want me to meet you so you're free to go if you need to get back to the hospital?"

"No, he's doing well. I feel much better about him. I'll pick you up at seven and I can't wait."

"I can't, either," she said, though she could barely get her breath, her throat had tightened with so much emotion. If she was like this now, how would she get through tonight when she was with Wade?

"I'll see you then," he said. "Make it six thirty. That way we'll be through dinner sooner and we can go back to my condo if Dad is doing okay."

"That's fine," she said, hurting and wanting to be with him and have his strong arms around her.

"See you then," he said, adding a goodbye and he was gone.

After tonight he would be out of her life. She put her head in her hands and cried because that thought hurt so much. And that's when she realized that her biggest fear had come true. She had fallen in love with Wade, sooner than she had thought she would, more deeply than she had dreamed possible.

And tonight she had to say goodbye.

At six thirty that night, after she'd dressed for dinner in a red sweater and brown skirt, she wished she hadn't pulled her long, blond hair off her face in a low clip. Her heart hurt and knew the pain would just worsen when she saw Wade. How could she be this deeply in love with him in such a short time? She knew the answer to her own question. He was wonderful in so many ways. When his car came up the drive, she went to open the door.

He came up the porch steps two at a time and crossed the porch in long strides.

He wore jeans, another blue denim shirt and his boots. She opened the door and his gaze drifted slowly over her. "Whoa, look at you. You look better than any dinner possibly could," he said, stepping in and closing her door behind him. "It's been a hell of a day, but it's better now," he said, slipping his arms around her waist and leaning down to kiss her as he drew her into his embrace.

Her heart thudded and she forgot dinner and her resolution to tell him goodbye. She forgot everything except his mouth on hers and his arms around her and his hard, muscled body pressed against her.

She didn't know how long they kissed, but he picked her up and asked where the bedroom was and she pointed as she pulled his head down to kiss him.

He carried her to her bedroom and for the next hour he made love to her. Afterward, they lay in each other's arms as he lightly ran his hand through her hair, letting the locks slip and fall.

"You're so beautiful, Ava. I couldn't wait to be with you again, and dinner seemed insignificant, but if you'll throw on the same sexy outfit, I'll take you out to feed you."

"If you want something simple, I have burgers in the freezer. I can put them on the grill and we can eat here."

"Fine with me," he said as his arm tightened around her and he kissed her.

Soon they showered and dressed again.

"I'll get the grill and cook the patties if you want to do the other stuff," he offered.

"Sure," she said, taking him to her kitchen.

"Your house is nice," he said, glancing around a roomy kitchen with large windows that in the daytime would allow a lot of light on the yellow-and-white decor.

She showed him the grill on the patio that was under the limbs of big oaks. Through dinner she had no appetite for, they talked about his dad and the new rodeo arena being built.

"They'll have a big celebration when they have the grand opening next year. I'd like you to go with me."

She smiled at him, though his invitation brought her nothing but pain. "That's way too far in the future."

"So that's a no." It wasn't a question.

"It's a 'that's too far in the future,'" she said. Trying to defer further questions, she diverted his attention from the invitation. "Will you perform in the rodeo?"

"No, I won't. I haven't competed in a rodeo for several years. But I like to watch them." He looked down at her plate. "You're not eating. Is something wrong?"

She knew this was the time to tell him. "Let's go inside to talk. I'll get these dishes later."

"I can help right now and we'll be through in no time," he said, carrying their dishes to the sink.

She caught his wrist. "C'mon. Let's talk."

They walked into her family room, a room with lots of big windows that let in the east light and gave a view of her flowerbeds filled with roses that still bloomed.

She sat on the sofa and he sat facing her. "What's the problem, Ava?"

She hoped she could get through this without getting emotional. "Wade, it's been wonderful with you. I've enjoyed every minute. But this is one of those good things that has to come to an end. I don't want to get hurt again and this time I think I might get hurt worse than I did by my ex-fiancé."

"This is because of my views of marriage and children, isn't it?" he asked, looking intently at her.

"Yes, it is. You don't want marriage and you don't ever want kids. You're very firm about that."

"Yes, I am. I blame Wynn for Dad's heart problems. He's worried our dad to pieces."

"I imagine you feel more strongly about it after today and your dad being in the hospital for his heart."

"As a matter of fact, yes, I do," he said, looking somber.

"On the other hand, I want to marry and I want kids. I think I need to say goodbye and get out of your life now before I'm hopelessly in love with you and have to say these words and hurt way more. This isn't something where we can reach an easy compromise."

"No, it sure as hell is not." They gazed at each other in silence for minutes and she hurt more than she had thought she would. She stood to move away from him and his dark eyes that seemed to look right through her. She fought back tears and waited to talk until she could get her emotions under control.

She turned to face him. "I think we need to stop seeing each other completely. I can't take intimacy lightly. I've said what I need to say and tonight has to be goodbye." Clenching her teeth, she fought back tears.

He stood looking at her and after a moment he nodded. "I don't want to tell you goodbye, but I don't want to hurt you, either. I didn't want to hurt you this much."

"You let me know how you felt. I went out with you, anyway, so that's on me."

He said nothing for a moment, his eyes downcast, then slowly nodded his head. "I don't like it and I don't want to say goodbye, but I understand." His eyes met hers and she saw the anguish there that matched her own.

She watched as he turned to walk to the front door. Struggling more than ever to hold back tears, she went to the door right behind him. He opened the door, then turned to face her and he frowned.

"You've been wonderful and I've hurt you. I never wanted to do that."

"I know you didn't," she said. "It's no one's fault, Wade. We're just poles apart in our views of love and marriage and kids."

"We damn sure are, so this is best," he said gruffly. A muscle worked in his jaw and he looked tense. "You've seen my brother in action, so I hope you can understand where I'm coming from."

"Wade, I'll never understand. Family is the best part of life—love of a spouse, children, relatives. That's what I want with all my heart and I can't imagine deliberately cutting yourself out of a lifetime of joy just because of escapades by your twin. If you married, you're different from your dad. The woman you marry will be different from your mom. Any kids you have will have different influences in their lives. I know he's given your dad, your siblings and you grief, but that doesn't mean any child you would have would ever be like your twin." She looked away, clenching her fists because he'd made this a protracted goodbye and she couldn't hold back her tears. They spilled down her cheeks.

"Dammit, I've made you cry and that I never wanted to do." He reached out and cupped her face, wiping her tears with his thumbs. "I wish this wasn't goodbye, but you're a beautiful, sexy, smart woman and I know you'll get over me."

Would she? Right now she doubted it. He was a good man, accomplished, caring, so handsome and sexy. She knew now she should have walked away sooner before she got hurt. Before she fell in love.

Once again, she tried to get a grip on her emotions. She shouldn't be feeling emotional over him. There had never been a declaration of love. They hadn't even known each other well enough or long enough to be deeply in love. She had to wipe away her tears and stand strong.

He tilted her face and looked at her. "I don't want it to be, but I guess this is goodbye," he said gruffly. He ran his fingers lightly on her cheek and lifted locks of her long hair away from her face. "You've been special," he said. "If you change your mind about the ranch or going out with me or just want to talk, you know how to reach me."

"I know." She brushed a kiss on his cheek and was going to turn and step away.

Instead his arm circled her waist and he held her tightly against him, putting his other arm around her and leaning her over, and he kissed her hard. A possessive, hot kiss that she knew she would remember forever. She shook in his arms and then she lost awareness of everything except his kiss, his mouth and tongue, his arms around her holding her tightly. While her heart pounded, she forgot all their problems because she was lost in the sexiest kiss of her life.

Finally he released her, both of them gasping for breath as they stared at each other.

"I'll never forget you," he said in a husky voice. Then he turned and went striding to his car.

She shut the door and stood there, unable to move. Tears streamed down her cheeks, but her silent, oh, so empty house reminded her why she had told him goodbye. She wanted a family man in her life, a man who loved babies and children, who would be a good dad.

It wasn't going to be Wade.

Putting her hands over her face, she cried because she was in love with him. So deeply in love with him. He was an ideal man in so many ways except the two most important things. She couldn't take life on his terms. He wouldn't take it on hers. Besides, he wasn't a man in love.

She had tried to minimize her feelings for him and what was happening in her life while he stayed at her cabin, but he had been too wonderful for her to guard her heart and resist him.

She sat in the nearest chair, placing her head in her hands, and let the tears fall freely.

"I love you, Wade Sterling," she whispered through her sobs. "I'll do everything in my power to get over you and forget you. I'm sure you'll forget me and you don't have to get over going out with me."

The worst part was, despite it all, she wanted to be in his bed, in his arms. She loved him. And she knew she would for the rest of her life.

# Eleven

As Wade drove away, he hurt. He wanted Ava in his arms tonight. He wanted to make love to her all through the night and he wanted to take her home to his ranch tomorrow and show it all to her.

His feelings for her astounded him. She had gotten closer to his heart than any other woman he had ever known.

He still hadn't changed his mind about marriage and children, and he never would. But that didn't stop him from missing Ava.

All he could think about was Ava, holding her, kissing her. Fabulous kisses that set him on fire and made him tremble from head to toe. But he'd never kiss her again. Now he had only one thing he could do. Get over her.

He realized she was the first woman about whom he'd had to tell himself that. He had always been able to end affairs with his heart intact—Olivia, for instance—and he told himself this wouldn't really be any different. He wasn't in love and whatever he felt for Ava, he could get over it. He had to.

The next day he left for the Bar S Ranch. He'd stayed in town unusually long and now that he looked back on the days in Dallas, he realized part of it was getting back after the storm and seeing his family, but he realized he had stayed in Dallas because Ava was there.

He couldn't get her out of his thoughts as easily as he expected, and last night had been long and lonely. All night he'd told himself he'd get over her, that there would be someone else in his life, but right now, he missed her and he was going back to his ranch, where hard work would take his mind off her.

He drove another pickup he kept in Dallas to replace the one that went into the creek. It had been found and the sheriff called this morning about it. His wallet had been found, too, in the pickup, and they were sending the dried contents back to him. He'd have to get all new cards. The last thing he did before he left Dallas was place a large order of wild Alaskan salmon to be shipped to Gerald and Molly, as well as four cakes from a famous Texas bakery in a small town near Dallas, to show his gratitude. A similar order went to Sheriff Ellison.

He wished there was a way to show his gratitude to

Ava, but their evening at the private dinner club would have to suffice. He wouldn't be seeing her again.

Opening the window of the pickup, he let the breeze blow away his memories of her.

At the ranch he poured himself into working outside. Sometimes he rode with the cowboys. He made repairs in the barn and he built a new dog house for a stray that had either wandered up or been dropped off.

The weekends were the worst and he tried to do enough physical work that he would go to bed exhausted and sleep would finally overtake him.

He had some women friends who lived in the ranch area. On a weekend he'd called one of them and she could go out for dinner and a good time.

Or so he thought.

The first Saturday night he went out, he just thought about Ava and took his friend home early. At her doorstep she turned to look at him. "I had a fun time tonight, but I don't think you did. We've known each other a long time, Wade. I heard your dad has been in the hospital and I thought he was doing fine. Is that what's worrying you?"

"No, Nan," he said, smiling at the redhead he'd known for years. She was a good friend. "I've just had things in my life that didn't go the way I wanted."

She laughed and punched his shoulder lightly, leaning closer to stare at him. "Are you in love with someone who walked out? It had to happen someday, even to you."

He laughed. "I don't think so. I'm not in love and I'm not a marrying man and you know that."

"I know that, but your heart might not. It's hard to feel sorry for you, though, because you're the one who breaks hearts and you've never had a clue what that feels like."

He shook his head as he smiled. "Okay, enough on that subject. Sorry if I wasn't my best tonight."

She kissed his cheek. "I never thought I'd see this day come. Buddy, you're in love and you don't even know it, or else you don't want to be. Well, you'll get over it like we all do. Thanks for tonight. See you around, my friend." She laughed as she went in her house and shut the door.

He walked back to his pickup and drove to the ranch. A big furry dog met him when he stepped inside the fence. "Hi, Buster," he said, scratching the dog's back. "Want to go down with the cowboys or come in with me?" He held the gate open. The dog sat and looked up at him. Wade jerked his head and walked toward his house, letting the dog in with him.

The big ranch house was empty, and as he walked through it, Buster his only companion, he envisioned Ava here. Sitting on the sofa in her skintight jeans and heels, her feminine touches all around the room. He couldn't stop thinking about her, wondering what she was doing. Was she thinking about him, or seeing some other guy already? He couldn't count the number of times each week he'd pulled out his phone and had to force himself not to call her.

He stalked into the kitchen, the noise of his boot heels the only sound in the house. In the cavernous void, he thought he heard the echo of Nan's remarks.

*You're the one who breaks hearts and you've never had a clue what that feels like.*

Nan was right about that. He'd always been able to say goodbye. But this time was different. This was the first time in his life he really missed someone. Not only did he hurt, but he also couldn't concentrate on work, which had never happened to him.

He'd worked long hours all week, coming in when it got dark and working in the barn or in his office until one or two in the morning. He hadn't slept well and he had no appetite at all.

He felt a tightening in his gut. Could Nan be right in her other assertion? Was he in love with Ava?

That thought shook him to the core.

"Damn," he said. He sat in a kitchen chair and scratched Buster's back, and groaned. How could she have gotten under his skin in such a short time? Especially when their views of life, love and the future were on opposite ends of the spectrum. He raked a hand through his hair and expelled a tight breath. He didn't know the answer to that, but he knew one thing for sure. If he had fallen in love, he'd get over it soon.

He pushed back the chair. "Time to work out, Buster. You want to come run on the treadmill? I tried to get her to come visit us, but she wouldn't. You'd like her and I'll bet she would like you. Damn, I miss her."

He left the room to go to his gym and work out until he could shake Ava out of his thoughts.

On a Sunday afternoon weeks later, when he was sitting at the table nursing a cup of coffee, one of the men called to tell him his brother Wynn just passed through the front gates. Wade thanked him and got his hat to walk out to the porch to wait. Wynn never came to the Bar S; he despised ranching, horses and everything about either one. Wade couldn't imagine why he was coming now. He wasn't going to try to guess. He sat in a white wooden rocking chair, put his feet on the rail and sat back to wait. Then Wade thought about their dad. Cold fear gripped him that something else had happened to his dad's heart.

He saw the plume of dust and then the bright red sports car speeding toward the house. Wynn hadn't changed since he was a teenager; he still liked fast cars. The car skidded to a stop, sending up a cloud of dust. Wynn didn't get out until the dust settled. He walked around the car and headed for the porch. His turquoise dress shirt was open at the throat and he didn't wear a tie. He had on charcoal slacks and loafers.

Wade's curiosity grew and so did his worry about his dad because Wynn definitely didn't look angry, he looked worried. Even if it was Dad, Wynn would have just called, he told himself, unless it was really terrible. Fear gripped him. "Is Dad okay?" he asked.

"As far as I know. That's not why I'm here."

Wade pushed out the breath he'd been holding, relieved. At least his dad was okay…but what did Wynn want?

"You must have an important reason to drive all the way out here," Wade said, assessing his brother. A muscle worked in Wynn's jaw and some emotion flashed in his dark eyes, but there was a hesitancy in his twin that Wade had never seen. Usually Wynn made his anger clear to all. Or his fear. Or his pleasure. He wasn't a subtle person and Wade's curiosity grew.

"Well, have a seat. We don't have to stand to talk," Wade said, sitting back in the rocker and turning it so he would face Wynn, who sat in another big rocker. Wynn sat on the edge of the seat and he looked nervous.

"You might as well say it," Wynn said. "You know I'm a dad."

"Oh, yes, I do," he said, briefly startled that the long-ago phone conversation was the reason for Wade's appearance.

"You didn't tell Violet it was you she was talking to that day."

"Violet? I did tell her, but she accused me of lying and we never got back to it. It was obvious you didn't tell her you're a twin, so after that first try I didn't, either."

They sat staring at each other and with every second, Wade became more and more puzzled because Wynn wasn't acting in his customary manner.

"You told Violet the check was in the mail and that's exactly what I would have told her because it was. That's how I found out you talked to her. She told me it was a good thing I wasn't lying when I said the check was in the mail."

"I was in shock and that sounded like what you'd say."

Wynn nodded, apparently accepting Wade's answer. He looked away for a moment, eyeing something in the distance, his hands toying with a rope that had been looped over the rocker.

Wade tilted his head, his curiosity growing. "You drove all the way out here for something. What's eating you?"

His brother finally looked at him. "You didn't tell the folks that they're grandparents. You haven't told anyone in the family. Why?"

Wade shrugged. "It's your secret and when I thought about it, I figured you were doing what you thought was best. I figured it might be better for Mom and Dad if they didn't know about this baby. It's really your call."

"I can't understand you. There was your chance for revenge for all the grief I've given you over the years. Real revenge. This could have wrecked my engagement to Olivia if you'd gone about it in certain ways."

"I'll be damned. You can't understand trying to do the right thing or the nice thing," Wade said, shocked that Wynn actually was puzzled why someone wouldn't do him harm. "Why in the hell would I want to deliberately hurt you? Damn, Wynn, to my way of thinking, life is a whole lot better and you have more friends being nice to people. You ought to try it sometime." He shook his head as Wynn continued to stare at him, obviously confused. "You're really at a loss about this, aren't you?"

"I know I've made you mad plenty of times. Absolutely furious."

"Yes, you have. That doesn't mean I'd enjoy doing

that to you. I don't get a thrill out of being mean and I don't seek revenge, either."

Wynn dropped the rope and sat back, but he said nothing. He just looked at his brother.

"You know, Wynn, for the first time in my life, I feel sorry for you. You don't even know what you're missing." They stared at each other and Wade thought if a creature had appeared from outer space, he wouldn't have been any more puzzled. But this was his blood brother; he had to try to reach him.

"You know, Wynn, as toddlers and little kids we fought constantly and we really never outgrew that, which is sad. You and I should be brothers, in the deepest sense of the word.

"You're my twin and we don't understand each other or like each other. We can't even sit out here and enjoy a cup of coffee together before you go. We have no common ground and that's sad."

"I took Olivia from you. She's the perfect woman—every man's dream. You're not angry over that?"

Wade stared at him a moment in silence as he gave a slow shake of his head. "No, Wynn. Olivia's a wonderful woman, but she's better suited to you." They sat quietly a moment. "You know, it's not too late to become real brothers. Do you want a cup of coffee?"

Wynn's eyes widened with surprise and he tilted his head as he stared at Wade. "You're serious, aren't you?"

"Yeah, I am. If Lucy was here, or Jack, I'd make that offer to them and we'd sit and chat. I would with Mom or Dad, too. The rest of us all enjoy each other's company and like to be together. That's family at its best. It's not too late for us to become real brothers."

Wynn blinked and nodded. "I suppose I could try… Okay, we'll have a cup of coffee together."

"Just sit there. I have some brewed. I'll bring it out."

He left, wondering if they could tolerate each other for ten more minutes. He was back with mugs on a tray that also held cream and sugar, spoons and napkins. He set the tray on a table between them.

"Well, this is a first," Wynn remarked with sarcasm in his voice.

"Yeah. We might as well give it a try."

Wynn picked up his mug and took a sip. "I guess I should say thank you because it's a relief to me that you'll keep my secret."

"Sure, Wynn," Wade replied. "You might try life my way sometime," he said, "and I don't mean by trying to pass yourself off as me."

"Olivia made me promise I wouldn't do that anymore," Wynn said, sounding more like himself and making Wade smile as he shook his head.

"She'll learn." Wade leaned forward and held out a hand to his brother. "I think it's wonderful that you and Olivia are in love. I truly wish you the best."

"You mean that, don't you?"

"Yes, I do. I'm sincere about everything I've said to you."

Wynn accepted the proffered hand and shook it.

Wade smiled as he gave a playful punch to his

brother's shoulder. "I can't believe my twin is getting married."

*Married...* At the mention of the word, his thoughts went to Ava. It'd been weeks, but still memories of her slammed into him. He couldn't seem to forget her.

Some men did—the guy that walked out on her. But he couldn't.

Wade drew a deep breath. He remembered how his heart beat faster and his whole body responded to just the sight of her. Her blue eyes melted him and if he saw her in the distance or across a room, desire consumed him. There was no way on earth he could see her the way he saw other women. She was gorgeous, special, unique. But she'd never be his, not the way Olivia would soon be Wynn's.

His brother's words drew him out of his reverie. "I may have to try life your way. I know how to act the part. Maybe I should try to live the part and see if I'm happier."

"You don't have to try to be like me," Wade said, focusing on Wynn again. "Just be considerate of your family and others. I think you'll find you have more people who like you. Life ought to be better. Start with your family and be nicer to them. As I just said, they bear the brunt of your anger and deceptions."

"They do. Anybody else would retaliate. Thanks again about the baby. I'll send her money until she's grown and educated. I'll do what's right."

"You're sure you don't want Mom and Dad to know their grandchild?"

"I'm sure. It's a baby girl, but no, I don't. Mom

and Dad would have nothing in common with the baby's mother."

"They would have a baby in common, Wynn."

He frowned and shook his head. They sipped coffee and sat in silence for a few minutes, Wynn deep in thought. "I'll think about it, Wade."

"Good. You won't regret letting them know their grandchild. I feel certain about that."

"I never looked at it that way. I didn't think they'd be happy about the mother."

"They might not, but I'll bet they'll love your baby. They might be a good influence on the mother."

"Wow. Maybe I will. You sound very positive."

"I am. It's your baby and their first grandchild. They will be happy. I know Mom and Dad."

"Well, maybe I should." He was silent for a few minutes. "I asked Mom why she married Dad—I'll still call him dad," Wynn said finally.

"I'm glad because in every way except blood, he's been our dad, and to me, he's our only dad. Why did she marry him?"

"She said she was single, pregnant, didn't have money to raise a child by herself and didn't want to. Dad started dating her and in his own quiet way, he loved her and asked her to marry him, so she did, but she's never told him the truth about getting pregnant. And she said that he was such a good man that it didn't take her long to fall in love with him, too. She said she realized she had found the best father for her twins."

Wynn set down his coffee mug and leaned forward. His eyes met Wade's and there was sincerity shining there. "Wade, that woman you had at the folks' house—Ava. She must have been important to you. In fact, if I'm not mistaken, I think you're in love with her."

"I am."

The words fell out of his mouth before he could even think, shocking the hell out of him. But he wouldn't retract them. He couldn't. Heaven help him, but there was no denying the truth. He was totally, irrevocably in love with Ava Carter.

"Then you need to go get her."

There, Wade took exception. No way could he just go back to Dallas and claim the woman he loved.

"Hell, I didn't do it the conventional way, but I went after the woman I wanted," Wynn said with a grin. "And now I'm getting married. It still amazes me, but I love Olivia. I can't imagine being a dad— even though technically I am one. But the thought of actually possibly raising a child, being a real dad day in and day out, scares me."

"Why?" Wade asked, curious what Wynn would fear.

"I don't know little kids. I wasn't good to Jack. I thought he was a nuisance."

"I imagine brothers are different than sons," Wade remarked, unable to imagine Wynn as a parent with real responsibilities.

Wynn stood. "I guess I'll get going." He put his coffee cup on the tray and turned to Wade. "Thanks again for keeping my secret."

Wade stood. "Sure, Wynn."

"Well, we got through a cup of coffee together, maybe we can get through lunch together sometime."

Wade nodded. "I'm willing to try. I'll see you in town in about a week. Meanwhile, take my advice and try being nicer to the family and see what happens. After all, family is the most important part of life."

Wynn nodded.

"I'll call you about lunch next week."

"Sure." Wynn went down the porch steps and walked to his car. Wade watched him go and wondered if he would really change.

Could he marry and have kids?

He'd just told Wynn that family was the most important thing—family meant a wife and kids. And love between a man and a woman. He loved Ava. He faced that now, full on. He knew why he'd been living with hurt and loneliness, missing her for the last three weeks. He was in love with her. Deeply in love. Was it enough to marry and have kids? he asked himself again.

Kids with Ava… Right now that sounded good to him. Being a dad. He couldn't imagine himself being a father unless it was with her.

He'd knew he'd have to accept children if he wanted her in his life. After all, she had shut him out and said goodbye in order to avoid heartbreak months or years down the road when they separated. Well, there was a better way to guard against getting another broken heart and his way was a lot better than her way.

He pulled out his phone to call Ava and tell her he was coming to see her.

# Twelve

Wade was coming over.

After three weeks, she was surprised he'd called, and she was still confused. He never gave a reason, just said he was coming. She wouldn't get her hopes up—after all, she was sure nothing had changed. She couldn't imagine that he had changed one tiny bit in his views. He was too set in them, and when his dad had had the last heart episode, Wade had become even more adamant that he didn't want to marry and have children.

She had gone back to work in Dallas as soon as she got home, and tried to keep as busy as possible because it helped to have less moments to herself, lonely moments when she remembered being in his arms, being with him. Nothing could stop her missing him and his vitality, his passionate lovemaking, his flirting. She missed him terribly and she loved him deeply, but she still would leave him the same way again. She might not ever love a man to the extent that she loved Wade, but she couldn't be in a relationship based on anything less than total commitment. And she would never give up her desire to marry and have children.

No matter the reason, he was coming to see her and she knew it wouldn't work out.

Even so, she had carefully applied makeup, put on a short-sleeved red dress with a V-neck and a full skirt that fell in folds below her waist. Her hair was tied back at her nape with a sheer red scarf and she had matching high-heeled pumps.

When she heard his car, she couldn't keep from going to the door. Her heartbeat raced. She tried to calm herself down because he could be coming for some ordinary reason and just be here minutes. When he rang the bell, she opened the door and her heart thudded.

He looked so incredibly handsome, so absolutely wonderful, dressed in a navy Western-cut suit, black boots and a white dress shirt with his usual French cuffs with gold cuff links. She wondered if she was going to love him the rest of her life and never marry because all men would pale in comparison. She wanted to throw herself into his arms and kiss him. Instead, she took a deep breath and, in a surprisingly modulated voice despite her pounding heart, said hello.

He looked at her. "Can I come in?"

"Oh," she gasped. She hadn't realized she was just standing there staring while she was fighting throwing herself into his arms. "Come in."

Smiling, curiosity in his eyes, he stepped inside, closed the door and turned to her. "You look gorgeous."

"Thank you. Come in and sit down," she said, walking into her front room. He followed and she turned to face him. "Have a seat."

"Thanks," he said, but he kept looking at her and didn't move. "I've missed you, Ava," he said.

"I've missed you, too." Her heart started drumming and she wondered what he had in mind. Why was he here? Why was he saying these things to her when he knew he was breaking her heart?

"Ava, I've been miserable without seeing you," he said so softly, she could barely hear him.

He took a step closer. "I don't know where to start. I've missed you. I love you. I'm miserable without you. You're the most important person in the whole world to me."

Her heart pounded but she couldn't give in to him again, no matter how much she wanted to echo his words. Not when their relationship had no future. She just stood there looking at him, seeing the desire in his eyes.

He stepped forward to wrap his arms around her. His voice was shaky when he spoke again. "I love you, Ava. I want to marry you. We can have kids. If you're their mother, they'll have to be wonderful."

Was she imagining this? For the past several weeks

she'd dreamed every night that he'd show up at her door and say these things to her.

"Ava, did you hear me?" He gripped her arms tighter and it was like a wake-up call.

Her heart surged.

"Do you mean that? You really want kids?" She twisted away slightly to look up at him. Amazement shook her, as well as hope.

"I want whatever makes you happy," he said. "If you want kids, then I want kids."

"You're sure?" she asked, her heart pounding as she held her breath. "That's something you have to be sure about."

"I'm sure. I don't want to live alone or live the way I have been without you. It was pure hell. We'll have all the kids you want. I have to have you in my life. Kids and all. Will you marry me?"

She couldn't keep from crying as he was talking and holding her. "I've missed you and I love you and yes, yes, I'll marry you," she said.

He leaned back to look at her and wiped her tears. "Why are you crying? We can have kids. I want to marry you."

He tightened his arms, leaned over her to kiss her and she knew that the love of her life was holding her tightly, kissing her, going to marry her and they would have the family she had dreamed about.

"I'm so happy," she said, sobbing with relief and joy and amazement as she clung to him and kissed him.

She felt bereft when he stepped out of her embrace

and went down on one knee. He dug something out of his pocket and looked up at her. "I love you, Ava Carter. I love you with all my heart. I can't live without you. Marry me and let's have all the babies you want. Ava, will you marry me?"

She was crying and laughing at the same time and she couldn't believe what he was saying, but she didn't doubt that he meant every word. Her heart pounded with joy. "You'll be okay with it if I want six kids?"

"I'll be overjoyed because I'll be with you. I love you, my darling, and I'll ask you again, will you marry me?"

"Yes, I'll marry you. I love you," she exclaimed.

He held out a box wrapped in white paper and tied with a pink bow. She took it and opened it, her heart drumming. She gasped and looked at him and then back at a gorgeous, huge diamond set in a gold band. "This is beautiful."

He stood and took the ring from her to slip it on her finger. She looked up into his dark eyes and she smiled. "I've missed you so."

"Not anywhere like I've missed you. I've been miserable. I was so scared I'd lost you forever. I love you with all my heart and want you in my life, in my arms always." He tightened his arms around her.

She looked down at her ring, then back up at him. "I've dreamed of this moment, I can't tell you how many times, but I never expected you to change your opinions on marriage and children. Why, Wade?"

"A man can change. Olivia has changed my brother,

and you've changed me." He told her about Wynn's visit to the ranch and how he seemed like a different man when he left the Bar S. "I realize there's truth to what you've been saying all along. Family is the most important thing. And our kids will be good people, just like you. I love you, Ava, and I'll never tire of calling you my wife and the mother of my children."

He kissed her then, a long, passionate kiss that made her feel totally wanted and loved. She clung to him, her heart pounding with joy, with love for him, with happiness for their future.

"I have one request," she said when she could manage to speak. "I want a wedding soon."

He smiled. "We won't interfere with the date Wynn and Olivia have picked—December twentieth—but I think we can make it a quick wedding. And I'll take you anywhere you'd like to go for a honeymoon."

"How about a wedding in early November?"

"That's fine with me." He chuckled. "That was easy."

"It's easy for me to pick a date because I don't have family to worry about."

"You do now, Ava." He picked her up in his arms, kissed her and carried her to her bedroom.

She clung to him as they kissed. He stood her on her feet and held her tightly. She opened her eyes to look at him and at her ring that glittered in the soft light. "Ah, I love you and you've made me the happiest woman on earth."

He laughed. "Have you stopped to think a minute about the future? Can you live on a ranch?"

"If it's with you, yes, I can. I might get that teaching certificate because I'll bet there's a little country school somewhere near your ranch where I could teach."

"As a matter of fact, there is. There's a little town with a school. Great idea."

"I'll keep my place near Persimmon for a retreat. A retreat that maybe we can fill with kids," she said, smiling at him.

He pulled her close. "I can't wait to show you the Bar S."

"Do you have a guest house?" she asked as he showered kisses on her ear and neck and nape while his hands moved over her.

"Yes, I have three guest houses."

"I want to invite Gerald and Molly to visit us."

"You can have anybody you want," he whispered and leaned back to look at her. "You're beautiful and I love you and you really have made me the happiest man on earth now."

"Wait until we have a family. You'll really know happiness then. It'll be good, Wade, I promise."

He laughed. "You can't promise that. There are no guarantees in life like that."

"Want to bet? Watch me. You'll be happy."

He laughed again until she pulled his head down to kiss him. She held him tightly while her heart pounded with joy. She would have the love of her life and she would have a family.

\* \* \* \* \*

*In the Return of the Texas Heirs series from*
USA TODAY *bestselling author Sara Orwig,*
*four rich ranchers return home to build*
*a new rodeo facility.*

*Look for all four stories!*
In Bed with the Rancher
One Wild Texas Night
*(available September 2020)*
*Luke's story and Cal's story,*
*coming March and April 2021!*

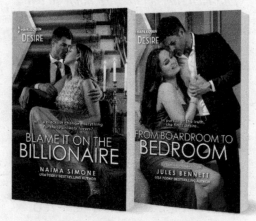

### #2755 TRUST FUND FIANCÉ

*Texas Cattleman's Club: Rags to Riches* • by Naima Simone

When family friend Reagan Sinclair needs a fake fiancé to access her trust fund, businessman Ezekiel Holloway is all in—even when they end up saying "I do"! But this rebellious socialite may tempt him to turn their schemes into something all too real...

### #2756 RECKLESS ENVY

*Dynasties: Seven Sins* • by Joss Wood

Successful CEO Matt Velez never makes the first move...until the woman who got away, Emily Arnott, announces her engagement to his nemesis. Jealousy pushes him closer to her than he's ever been to anyone. Now is it more than envy that fuels his desire?

### #2757 ONE WILD TEXAS NIGHT

*Return of the Texas Heirs* • by Sara Orwig

When a wildfire rages across her property, Claire Blake takes refuge with rancher Jake Reed—despite their families' decades-long feud. Now one hot night follows another. But will the truth behind the feud threaten their star-crossed romance?

### #2758 ONCE FORBIDDEN, TWICE TEMPTED

*The Sterling Wives* • by Karen Booth

Her ex's best friend, Grant Singleton, has always been off-limits, but now Tara Sterling has inherited a stake in his business and must work by his side. Soon, tension becomes attraction...and things escalate fast. But can she forgive the secrets he's been keeping?

### #2759 SECRET CRUSH SEDUCTION

*The Heirs of Hansol* • by Jayci Lee

Tired of her spoiled heiress reputation, designer Adelaide Song organizes a charity fashion show with the help of her brother's best friend, PR whiz Michael Reynolds. When her long-simmering crush ignites into a secret relationship, will family pressure—and Michael's secret—threaten everything?

### #2760 THE REBEL'S REDEMPTION

*Bad Billionaires* • by Kira Sinclair

Billionaire Anderson Stone doesn't deserve Piper Blackburn, especially after serving time in prison for protecting her. But now he's back, still wanting the woman he can't have. Could her faith in him lead to redemption and a chance at love? _____

*Billionaire Anderson Stone doesn't deserve
Piper Blackburn, especially after serving time in prison.
But now he's back, still wanting the woman he can't
have. Could her faith in him lead to redemption
and a chance at love?*

*Read on for a sneak peek at*
The Rebel's Redemption *by Kira Sinclair*

He had no idea what he was doing. But that didn't matter. The millisecond the warmth of her mouth touched his, nothing else mattered.

Like it ever could.

The flat of his palm slapped against the door beside her head. Piper's leg wrapped high across his hip. Her fingers gripped his shoulders, pulling her body tighter against him.

He'd never wanted to devour anything or anyone as much as he wanted Piper.

Her lips parted beneath his, giving him the access he desperately craved. The taste of her, sweet with a dark hint of coffee, flashed through him. And he wanted more.

One taste would never be enough.

That thought was clear, even as everything else in the world faded to nothing. Stone didn't care where they were. Who was close. Or what was going on around them. All that mattered was Piper and the way she was melting against him.

His fingers tangled in her hair. Stone tilted her head so he could get more of her. Their tongues tangled together in a dance that was years late. Her nails curled into his skin, digging in and leaving stinging half-moons. But her tiny breathy pants made the bite insignificant.

He needed more of her.

Reaching between them, Stone began to pop the buttons on her blouse. One, two, three. The backs of his fingers brushed against her silky, soft skin, driving the need inside him higher.

Pulling back, Stone wanted to see her. He'd been fantasizing about this moment for so long. He didn't want to miss a single second of it.

Piper's head dropped back against the wall. She watched him, her gaze pulsing with the same heat burning him from the inside out.

But instead of letting him finish the buttons, her hand curled around his, stopping him.

The tip of her pink tongue swept across her parted lips, plump and swollen from the force of their kiss. Moisture glistened. He leaned forward to swipe his own tongue across her mouth, to taste her once more.

But her softly whispered words stopped him. "Let me go."

Immediately, Stone dropped his hands and took several steps away.

Conflicting needs churned inside him. No part of him would consider pushing when she'd been clear that she didn't want his touch. But the pink flush of passion across her skin and the glitter of need in her eyes… He felt the same echo throbbing deep inside.

"I'm sorry."

"You seem to be saying that a lot, Stone," she murmured.

"I shouldn't have done that." He felt the need to say the words, even though they felt wrong. Everything inside him was screaming that he should have kissed her. Should have done it a hell of a long time ago.

Touching her, tasting her, wanting her was right. The most right thing he'd ever done.

But it wasn't.

Piper deserved so much more than he could ever give her.

*Don't miss what happens next in…*
The Rebel's Redemption *by Kira Sinclair.*
*Available September 2020 wherever*
*Harlequin Desire books and ebooks are sold.*

Harlequin.com

**IF YOU ENJOYED THIS BOOK
WE THINK YOU WILL ALSO LOVE**

# ⊕ HARLEQUIN

# PRESENTS

*Escape to exotic locations where passion knows no bounds.*

Welcome to the glamorous lives of royals and billionaires,
where passion knows no bounds. Be swept into a world
of luxury, wealth and exotic locations.

**8 NEW BOOKS AVAILABLE EVERY MONTH!**

# *Love Harlequin romance?*

## DISCOVER.

Be the first to find out about promotions, news and exclusive content!

**f** Facebook.com/HarlequinBooks

**🐦** Twitter.com/HarlequinBooks

**📷** Instagram.com/HarlequinBooks

**📌** Pinterest.com/HarlequinBooks

ReaderService.com

## EXPLORE.

Sign up for the Harlequin e-newsletter and download a free book from any series at **TryHarlequin.com**

## CONNECT.

Join our Harlequin community to share your thoughts and connect with other romance readers!
**Facebook.com/groups/HarlequinConnection**